DEVON LIBRARIES

MU OK DEVO
Please return/rene
Renew on te
www.dev

GW00507677

AP

Death to Owlhoots

Dave Markham had spent three years as a bounty hunter in his quest to build up a stake. Now he had returned to his roots and bought his own spread. Also figuring in his plans was the girl, Mabel North, whom he had known in his youth and now hoped to marry.

Markham discovers that he has bought trouble when the vendor of his ranch is revealed as a crooked blackmailer. Surviving a bushwhacking, Markham finds that he has a rival in both love and business in Jervis Manley, owner of the neighbouring Double J Ranch.

But an even greater danger comes from the sinister outlaw Slick Sadman, and Markham must buckle on his guns once again to fight for his life. But could he win through?

By the same author

Destined to Die

Death to Owlhoots

NORMAN LAZENBY

A Black Horse Western

ROBERT HALE · LONDON

© Norman Lazenby 1949, 2003
First hardcover edition 2003
Originally published in paperback as
Death to Owlhoots by Norman Lazenby

ISBN 0 7090 7382 8

Robert Hale Limited
Clerkenwell House
Clerkenwell Green
London EC1R 0HT

The right of Norman Lazenby to be identified as
author of this work has been asserted by him
in accordance with the Copyright, Designs and
Patents Act 1988.

All characters and events in this book are
fictitious and imaginary, and bear no
relation to any living person.

Typeset by
Derek Doyle & Associates, Liverpool.
Printed and bound in Great Britain by
Antony Rowe Limited, Wiltshire

ONE

CLOVERLEAF COWBOY

Right round the pole corral the cowboys sat, watching with narrowed humorous eyes as a youngster risked his limbs to tame a wild one. Right in the middle of the impromptu show, Dave Markham rode into the buildings of the Double J. He reined in his own gelding, watched the youngster with critical eyes. But he soon felt admiration for the youngster's work.

The kid was taking the bucks out of the bronc. He sat up in the saddle, his lean body rolling skilfully with every jerk of the wild animal. The bronc tore up the earth in its rage as it tried to throw the man from its back. There was madness and hatred in every savage kick and twist.

5

The young fellow had long since lost his hat. His black crisp hair was being powdered with the grime the wild one turned up. Little ripples of wind carried away the dust, so that the show was not obscured. The youngster stuck it, and in the end the bronc was whipped.

The animal knew it. They always knew when they had found a master. The tamed bronc changed quickly, almost incredibly. It settled down, stood with all four feet in the dust, blowing and snorting, shaking its head. Then the young cowhand trotted it meekly round the corral, while a burst of applause came from the onlookers. Dave Markham was able to get a better view of the young fellow, and he knew it was the man he had travelled many miles to see. Young Frank Manley had not changed much in the last three years. He was still a daredevil, six-foot chunk of manhood.

Dave chuckled. Frank had not seen him ride into the ranch yet. He had not seen his bosom pal of three years ago.

'Wal, that wasn't much of a scrap,' drawled Frank Manley to the cowhands. 'He's pretty tame now. Another two or three days and I reckon he'll be tamer than an ol' rockin' horse!'

'Ha, ha, ha!' There was a roar from the cowhands at this sally from their young boss.

And then an amazed look shot across Frank's face as he saw the mounted man.

'Say – it can't be! Dave Markham, of all people.

6

Wal, git down off that hoss, you son of a gun!'

Dave climbed down, scrambled through the poles of the corral, his batwing chaps flopping and his spurs ajingle.

They slapped each other across the back – with plenty of gusto!

'We've heard about yuh, Dave! Yes, sir, we heard all them tales. Three years of gun-toting against those badmen. You must have had a great time!'

'I'm not so sure,' said Dave quietly. 'I kinda missed the Double J – and your brother, Jervis. How is he?'

'Oh – fine, fine.' But there was a shade of uncertainty in Frank's voice. Dave noted it.

'And how is Mabel North?'

'She's fine, Dave.'

Dave took out the makings and began to roll the cigarette.

'She's isn't married?' he asked casually.

Frank grinned.

'Not yet. But there has been a lot of male visitors to the Double J. But not this past six months.'

'Why not, Frank?'

The other hesitated.

'Wal, Dave, I wouldn't say this to anyone but you – but Jervis has got himself strong-armed with ideas about Mabel. He's kinda unsympathetic to any galoot who shows up just for the idea of talking to Mabel.'

Dave Markham still smiled genially, but an

awkward silence fell between as they made their way to the ranch house set among the sheltering pepper trees. A gentle breeze came from the distant hills, dispelling the hint of early summer heat.

Mabel North had grown up as a little girl at the Double J. Her father had been a lifelong friend of Frank and Jervis's father, and when the girl had been made an orphan Tom Manley had seen to it that she did not lack a home. They had all grown up together – with Dave Markham starting work at the Double J in his early teens. That was when Tom Manley had died in a stampede accident, and left the ranch to his sons, Frank and the elder son Jervis.

Then Frank blurted it out.

'Truth to tell, Dave, I'm worried about Jervis. He's got so moody and mean this past year that no one can talk to him. Like as not he'll try to swing a fist at yuh. We've lost one or two of the old hands lately through his temper. Did you see Lash Logan at the corral? He's our new tophand. Tom Bailey quit after a row with Jervis. I was sorry about that. A mighty fine man, Tom.'

'I've been away three years, Frank. You forget I don't know this Lash Logan.'

'You soon will,' said the other gloomily. 'You figure to work for us, Dave?'

'Nope. I'm buying myself a spread – right here in this valley. What do you think of that, bronc-buster?'

Frank was puzzled.

'In the valley?' he yelped. 'But say, there ain't no spreads for sale!'

'Sure is. I made a deal with Thatch Gillman. Right up at the end o' the valley, on the other side of your fence. Gillman wants to quit – he wouldn't say why. I guess he reckons to book a permanent seat in the saloon. He doesn't like work.'

'Gillman's spread – the Lazy Cloverleaf!' Frank halted, momentarily nonplussed.

'Sure. Anythin' wrong with it? You look kinda fazed.'

'You surprised me. It's just that Jervis and Gillman have been at loggerheads for a long time now.'

'They never loved each other, I reckon.'

'But this is different, Dave. At one time it seemed they were actually on speaking terms, but now they're like two ornery old bulls.'

'Maybe they'll get over it. Some waddies are like that. They see each other on the range, in the town, kinda get a little touchy about something and there you are.'

Frank was doubtful.

'Sure would like to think it is as little as that. Come right in and see Jervis. He's in the ranch-house now.'

They mounted the steps and crossed the porch. Dave Markham noted the Double J was well-tended, with a good lick of paint all round. There were no broken fences; everything was in apple-pie order.

Three years ago Jervis Manley was likeable enough, though Dave had never been his special pal. Jervis had always been a one for worrying about the Double J. Dave wondered just how much real change he would find in the man.

He found that Jervis hardly smiled in greeting, though he shook hands cordially enough. Jervis looked a great deal older than Frank or Dave. Hard work round the ranch seemed to have made its mark – or maybe it was worry, secret worries. There was a querulous look on his thin bronzed face, and his shoulders had taken on a stoop. Dave was surprised at the changes he noted. Changes could come to a man gradually, and few of those around him notice it much. But a returning friend saw many things.

It was when Dave mentioned buying the Lazy Cloverleaf spread that Jervis actually scowled.

'So that hellion Gillman is running out,' he snapped.

Dave smiled.

'Well, I'm taking over, Jervis. Gillman will disappear into the Last Chance Saloon at Pine City.'

'That pack rat has some of my stock – hidden among the foothills, I guess. I've been there but I couldn't track them. He only registered the Lazy Cloverleaf brand because he could rustle Double J beef and alter the brand easily!'

So that was Jervis Manley's gripe! Dave stared back quietly. 'There's very little stock on the ranch,' he said. 'Gillman sold everything but about a hundred steers – he was pressed for money, he told me.'

'That rustler has plenty of money,' flung Jervis. 'And if you bought a hundred steers, you probably bought rustled Double J stock.'

'I took a look at some of Gillman's beef – naturally – and that cattle never had their brands worked over,' stated Dave.

'I think different!' shouted Jervis. 'And maybe I'll be coming over for that beef.'

'Come over. If you find a steer with a worked-over brand, you can have it. But why don't you take this up with Gillman, Jervis?'

'He's a double-crossin'—' began Jervis, and then checked his words. 'Damn Gillman! Reckon you're the mug if yuh bought rustled cattle. I'll be over, I tell you!'

'Sure, why not?'

Dave saw the other's eyes flick down at the silver-mounted gun Dave wore atop of his lean thigh. It was just a glance, but the lines on Jervis's face grew deeper.

'Say, Jervis, yuh never told me you blame Gillman for our missing stock,' declared Frank. 'At one time yuh reckoned it was Slick Sadman and his gang who had found a trail through the hills down the valley.'

'It was Gillman,' snapped Jervis. He clumped round the big living-room, scowled down at an Indian rug.

'That so? Wal, how does Charlie Kennedy account for his missing steers? These past few months, we all blamed Slick Sadman. The foothills lead into Charlie's Happy S spread, just like all the other outfits in the valley.'

'Listen, Frank,' said Jervis tensely. 'I'm running the Double J, as the old man wished, an' I got reasons to think Gillman took our steers. I got nothing to say about the rannies who rustled the Happy S range. Now Dave Markham comes bustin' along, says he's bought Thatch Gillman's outfit, lock, stock and barrel. I say he's also bought some of my beef.'

'Guess I'll git along,' said Dave suddenly. 'I'm ready to settle this argument over at my ranch any time. You come over and have a look-see.'

'Maybe it would be a good idea if you done away with the Cloverleaf iron,' said Jervis thickly. 'Register another brand. The Double J can be worked over with a running iron to a Cloverleaf too durn easy.'

Dave paused at the door.

'You can take it from me the new owner of the Lazy Cloverleaf don't hanker for any tricks like that,' he said humorously. He nodded to Frank, and stepped out.

Dave was going across the hard dirt to the hitching rack where he had tethered his gelding when a girl appeared just round the end of the ranchhouse. Dave altered stride and came up to her. She stood still under the pepper tree, and her lips parted in a delighted smile. She was a slim girl with golden tints in her brown hair. On her shirt was embroidered her name, 'Mabel.' But Dave would have known her had he never seen her for fifty years. Whenever the going had been tough and his last moments seemed inevitable, she had crept unaccountably into his thoughts. He had known Mabel since she was a kid.

'Dave Markham!'

He swept off his hat, took her hand vigorously.

'Why, Mabel North! Prettier than ever, I do declare.' Dave smiled into her eyes. They were bluer than the Arizona sky in summer. 'You're just the same – pretty much the same, so the *hombres* round here tell me.'

'So you've been asking about me!' she rippled.

He grinned.

'Wal, I jest got to ask about my old friends. I've bought a spread right here in the valley – the Lazy Cloverleaf. I sure think that brand is going to be lucky.'

'So Gillman is going!' she exclaimed. 'I'm glad. I hated that man. There has been something between him and Jervis, and look at Jervis now – so mean! He's got troubles, Dave.'

He nodded in agreement, privately thinking

that maybe Jervis Manley's troubles were mostly within his mind.

'So you're still around the Double J?' he repeated.

'I help Jervis and Frank. There is always something to do.'

'Sure hope Jervis doesn't keep yuh too busy. Like to ride over sometime – talk about old times.'

'You make us sound pretty old-timers!' she laughed. 'Anyway, I'm always glad to see a friend.'

He held her eyes, and she coloured slightly. Without words he was telling her he meant to be a very special friend.

While they were talking Jervis walked out on to the ranch-house porch. He stared stonily at the girl and Dave. So long was his stare that his attitude was definitely insolent.

But Dave Markham was not rattled. He had the easy assurance of a man who could retain his confidence in every situation.

'Like to see the deed to the Lazy Cloverleaf, Mabel?' he asked.

Just for the hell of it he would show Jervis that Mabel North was not his property yet.

'You have the deed?'

'Right here in my vest pocket. Gave Thatch Gillman cash for his spread.'

'You must have done right well on your travels, Dave?'

'I picked up a lot of reward money hunting bad

men,' he said briefly. 'Here's the deed, Mabel. I've got to get into Pine City and file this deed with the county clerk. Guess I should have done the job yesterday, but I figured I would ride round by the Double J and say howdo. This little scrap of paper makes me a rancher, Mabel.'

'I'm really glad,' she breathed. 'It'll give you a stake in the valley. A man has to have roots. You didn't really like gunslinging, did you, Dave?'

'I guess I wanted to work the wildness out of my blood. There were plenty of bad galoots to work on in Texas. Now I aim to settle down and raise a stock o' beef – small but plenty good. Yuh know that Gillman never worked the Lazy Cloverleaf rightly. There's good grass and water.'

'Maybe Jervis will straighten out a little now that Gillman is out of business,' said Mabel.

'Yuh think a lot of Jervis?'

'I like everyone around here. Jervis is my boss and a good friend.'

That was all he wanted to know. Mabel was not in love with Jervis Manley.

'Wal, I'll be over again, Mabel.'

He set his fifty dollar Stetson back on his head, and walked over to the gelding. He leaped to the saddle, waved to the girl and then at Jervis on the porch, and lightly touched the horse with his spurs.

His next stop would be the County Building in Pine City.

TWO

RUSTLER'S RUSE

Dave Markham rode westward across rolling range, down to Pine City at the mouth of the vast wide valley. In the distance the hills looked blue and misty. It was mostly good prairie with broken ground here and there. A few miles from Pine City were some timbered brakes, near the creek that watered all this range in the valley.

He wondered how it would all pan out – his intention to quit a wandering, gun-slinging life and settle down to respectable ranching. The little animosity between Jervis and him would soon be ironed out. There was no reason why he should not sink his roots deep into his own soil. Maybe get himself a wife. What was a rancher without a wife?

It was hard to believe that three years had slipped by since he last rode this way. The contour of the land was breaking as he neared the timbered brakes. His gelding picked a way through a rocky pileup. It was a wagon track to a shallow crossing of the creek.

It was while rounding a rocky shoulder that the rifle shot rang out. The warm, sunny stillness was shattered by the one shot. The bullet winged past his ear. He reined rapidly and his hand dropped for the silver-mounted gun with the slickness of constant practice. His fingers closed on the butt in a second.

Another second and the weapon would have been out, but another rifle shot sung out.

He did not even hear that report. He did not even hear the bullet whine. For the slug had scraped past his ear, taking skin and hair and leaving a scar that only time would heal. His head felt as if it were exploding like T.N.T.

All he could feel was pain and enveloping blackness. He slipped from the saddle, and the pain faded out. He never knew he hit the ground.

But returning consciousness brought with it an agonising splitting head. He groaned. He tried to lift himself, seeing nothing with pain-dazed eyes. He felt as if he could vomit, and his arms were ridiculously weak. He sank back to the ground, nursing his strength for a real effort to pull himself together.

When he finally sat up, he cursed. He cursed all bushwhackers in general.

'The yellow-backed rattler! The dirty snakeroo! Now who the hell would want to bushwhack me?'

There was no answer to these ruminations. He staggered down to the creek, doused his head in the cool water. It revived him no end, and although blood still came from the scar above his ear, he felt better. He found a handkerchief in his saddle-bag, and he tied it round his head. He returned, picked up his Stetson, looked at it.

'No holes. Good job that ranny didn't bore a hole in this hat. That might have made me real mad.'

His gelding was grazing at the end of trailing reins. He climbed on, this time without his usual litheness. His head swam sickeningly, but once in the saddle he felt a lot better.

As he sat tall in the saddle, he patted his pockets where he kept a small amount of money. It was still there. So robbery was not the motive. His fingers instinctively strayed to his vest pocket where the deed to the Lazy Cloverleaf lay.

Not a man to startle easily, he nevertheless spent several seconds running through his pockets and even the pouch in his belt. In the first second, of course, he knew the deed had vanished. The bushwhacker had taken that and nothing else.

Who on earth could it be? Who would want the deed to the Lazy Cloverleaf?

He searched round the rocky shoulder where he had been attacked. He was looking for tracks. He found them easily enough, and also the prints of a horse's hoof. The bushwhacker would be well away now.

Grimly, Dave climbed on the gelding. He knew exactly what he intended to do. If someone thought he could be gypped out of the ownership of the Lazy Cloverleaf, they were making one darned big mistake.

He galloped along the trail by the creek, and presently came to Pine City. It was a criss-crossing of dusty streets, just like a thousand other towns in the West. Frame buildings and hitching rails lined the streets. Saloons, honky-tonks and a few loafers seemed all that was visible. Dave rode on until he came to the courthouse. It was a big wood and brick building, right in the centre of the town.

It was good chance that he saw the sheriff on the cinder path to the courthouse. He noted the glint of sun on the metal pinned to the man's vest. He was an oldster. Pine City boasted its pride in its lawfulness. They did not need a fighting sheriff, it seemed.

'Yuh're just the man I want, sheriff,' began Dave. He pointed to his bandaged head. 'Some varmint bushwhacked me down by the coulees on the creek. That ain't all – he stole a deed to the possession of the Lazy Cloverleaf. I bought that deed off Thatch Gillman.'

'Have you a bill o' sale?' queried the sheriff.

'It was pinned with the deed.'

'Then you'll have to get another bill o' sale, mister. From Gillman – if he'll give it yuh. Strikes me yuh can't claim possession if yuh got no deed or bill o' sale.'

'Thanks,' said Dave grimly. 'I'm only telling yuh, because I reckon I can stomp my own snakes. I'm informing yuh, because you're the law. Understand? Likewise I've got something to tell the county clerk.'

He stamped his way in, down a corridor to the office.

A shrivelled little man was turning the pages of a ledger at a desk. There was another man in the room, with his back to Dave Markham. Dave knew it was Thatch Gillman. The man's enormous, bear-like shoulders were clad in a dirty, stained shirt. He wore a gun, but the holster was little used. Gillman, for all his gun-toting, did not practice much. A foolish sort of idea.

The clerk behind the desk was saying:

'Yes, now let me see, Mr. Gillman. What did yuh say about a ranch? I didn't quite ketch yuh words. Can't hear so well these days.'

But the little clerk's eyesight was good enough – at least to tell him that a newcomer had entered the room. He looked towards Dave. Gillman must have caught the glance, for the huge man wheeled suddenly.

A twisted smile spread over his dirty, whiskered face when he saw Dave.

'Howdy, Markham. You got business here?'

'Y-ea-h.' Dave paused, eyed the clerk. 'After yuh, Gillman.'

'Aw, I only wanted to ask about the free range in Tacoma Valley. It can wait.'

'Tacoma Valley ain't my territory, Mr. Gillman,' shrilled the little clerk. 'Reckon you oughta know that. Yuh bin round these parts long enough.' And the little wizened man cackled loudly.

Dave saw that Gillman was ready to step out, so he said his words.

'Would yuh tell me if any galoot has been in here to try and file a deed giving title to the Lazy Cloverleaf?' he asked the clerk. 'Because a deed was stolen from me. I figure the *hombre* who stole it thinks he can forge a bill of sale and claim the ranch. Or maybe deny the spread was ever sold.' Dave turned a grim face to Gillman with the last words.

Thatch Gillman's face went red with rage.

'Looky here, Markham, I see what yuh mean by them words, an' yuh can take it from me I never stole yuh deed.'

'I'm sure yuh didn't,' said Dave quietly, 'because I've got a bullet for the man who shows up with it. If he's got nerve to try and file claim on the spread, he's sure looking for a place on Boothill.'

There was fury and doubt in Gillman's ugly eyes. He was not a promising specimen of a rancher. He was more like a range tramp.

'I'm sure sorry tuh hear you lost that deed, Markham.'

'Too bad, ain't it? But maybe I can get a copy off the clerk – if you put it in writing that I paid yuh good cash for that spread. You'd sure do that tuh help me, Gillman. '

The man seemed to choke before he said with difficulty: 'Sure. Mighty pleased tuh help – yuh gave me a fair price.'

But Dave knew the man was lying. Dave made a good guess that Gillman was here at the court-house to deposit the Lazy Cloverleaf deed for safe keeping, receiving a receipt. Anyone who tried to claim the ranch without documentary proof would be bucking the law. And that was no good in Pine City.

So Gillman had sold him the ranch, taking his hard-earned cash, and then stealing back the deed. With the deed, Gillman could have laughed in Dave's face, especially if Dave could not produce a bill of sale. But Gillman's courage only went so far. He did not dare deny selling Dave the ranch. He had admitted the sale in front of the county clerk.

'I reckon we can git pen and paper right here,' drawled Dave. 'And maybe a copy of the deed. Should be a duplicate in this courthouse.'

And so Thatch Gillman was made to sign another bill of sale. He may have been good with a rifle as a bushwhacker, but his nerve had failed him when face to face with the man he had tried to swindle.

Dave came out of the courthouse feeling pleased with himself. He had a duplicate of the deed and another bill of sale bearing Gillman's signature. True he had a scar on his head, and he realised Gillman was an enemy. A dirty bush-whacker would try to even the score sooner or later.

Dave did not wonder that Jervis Manley was at loggerheads with Gillman, for the latter was a bad *hombre*. It was curious, however, that Jervis had let himself get so mean about his troubles.

Out in the street Dave encountered the sheriff of Pine City again.

'I've got that matter settled, sheriff. Got a new deed and a bill of sale. See here? Sure would like you to witness it, in case some snakeroo tries to drygulch me again.'

He showed the sheriff the papers.

'Glad you got fixed up, Mr. Markham,' said the sheriff.

Dave had a copy. The real deed was filed in the county clerk's office. His title to the Lazy Cloverleaf was secure.

Dave went home to the Lazy Cloverleaf that night, and before he turned in to bunk in the ranch-house he took a walk round the buildings, the barn and the corral. In the twilight it looked good.

Better than it looked by day, he knew. For Gillman had neglected the place somewhat. A good lick of paint would make a deal of difference, and a few days' work for a good carpenter would create an improvement. The ranch-house was small, and needed a good scouring. It would certainly get just that. If it was too small, it could easily be enlarged. Dave was dreaming a little, and he wondered why he should think the ranch-house small. It was big enough for one man!

But he knew he had something else in mind. Since meeting Mabel North that day, certain fanciful ideas were stirring in his head!

With more stock on the spread, he could build up to be a powerful rancher in the valley. He'd have to hire more hands. Two men had left with Thatch Gillman, and Dave had fired one on the spot. They were an untidy lot, as he had known at first glance. Only one of Gillman's men had stayed on – and he was an old drifter who had just started for Gillman. The old galoot was a wrinkled, tough old *hombre* to whom Dave had taken an instant liking.

He paused under the shade of a big cottonwood. A moon was riding high. It was a perfect night. He wished he had someone to talk to. The old drifter – Ned Brant – was asleep. He seemed to like his sleep.

Dave lit a cigarette, and used a match to light it. As the big-headed match spluttered, a bullet whined through the air and hit the tree bole.

Dave dropped to a crouch instantly. He cupped the cigarette. His gun whipped out, and he stared out over the range.

He thought he saw a movement, and then he was certain. The dull clomp-clomp of a horse's shoes echoed dully through the night. He dimly saw a figure hastily mounting the cayuse.

Dave knew the attacker had used a rifle and was a bit out of range of a .45. But he slung hot lead after the rider. The man was desperately spurring the animal into a gallop. Dave ran forward, in an effort to reduce the distance, but the other had the advantage. Dave stopped, fired two more shots and then shook his head.

The other man had escaped. But if his intention had been murder, he had failed.

'Twice in one day!' muttered Dave, as he walked back to the ranch-house. 'Could it be that varmint Gillman?'

He wondered at the logic of Gillman's animosity. It seemed the man just hated him because he had bought a ranch the other had been unable to make pay.

Ned Brant was on the steps of the bunkhouse, hitching up his pants belt.

'Was yuh shootin' coyotes or did I hear a hoss gallop away?' yapped the old-timer.

'It was a two-legged coyote,' said Dave. 'Better get that sleep of yourn, Ned. We're going on a ride round the spread tomorrow. I want to check up on the cows.'

But he and Ned had to ride far into the foothills the next day before they found the small herd. Dave wondered why the beef should be so far away from the creek. They had certainly moved a long way in twenty-four hours.

He had suspicions. He searched the trail and found evidence of his suspicions. Away from the marks made by the herd, he found imprints of one shod horse. There was certainly no more than one horse. The cattle had been on the move all night, and a nighthawk had been prodding them on.

'Someone has been getting at these cows,' he muttered. 'Though why he should drive them so far and leave them beats me.' He moved among the herd, examining the brands one by one. They were all Cloverleaf. He and Ned checked up on fifty. They found another fifty among a patch of timber, and again the brand was quite clear. Not one of these cows had been worked over with a running iron. Jervis Manley's accusations were unfounded – so far as this beef was concerned.

Of course, Gillman may have rustled some of the Double J cows, but Dave had bought only this hundred along with the ranch. Jervis ought to have it out with Gillman, and not get at the new owner of the Lazy Cloverleaf.

'I want this herd nearer the creek, Ned,' he stated. 'I wonder who the heck was the *hombre* who prodded them all this way?'

'Maybe some rustler,' suggested Ned Brant.

'Kinda senseless to prod them all night and then leave them.' Dave was about to leave Ned the job of driving the small herd further down the range when he saw three riders moving over the top of a hump. He recognised in the lead the lean shape of Jervis Manley.

Jervis wore a stern expression as his horse came up.

'I've come to look them steers over,' he said.

Dave sat calmly.

'Welcome, Jervis.'

He and Ned sat while the three riders nosed their horses among the cattle, examining the steers. It did not take long. Finally Jervis jigged his horse along to Dave. There was a baffled look on his face.

'I admit it – you're right. Those cows never had any brand but the Cloverleaf.'

'Thought yuh'd see it thataway, Jervis. If yuh think Gillman rustled Double J cows why don't yuh get after him?'

'It would be useless now,' gritted Jervis. 'The hellion has sold everything.' Jervis sat his horse uncomfortably. 'Yuh think the Double J is doing fine, don't yuh, Markham? Wal, let me tell yuh I got worries. Last year was not so good and I – wal, I got mixed up in some bad business.'

'Sure sorry to hear that, Jervis.'

'I got to thinking last night,' burst out Jervis. 'Seeing we're going to be neighbours we might as well get off to a decent start. Sorry to hear yuh had bushwhacker trouble yesterday.'

'Yesterday and last night. I suppose the news would get around. I think the same jigger tried to get me last night. That *hombre* and me have a score to settle some day.'

'Reckon who it might be?'

'Almost sure it was Gillman. Guess he resents me buying his ranch!'

At the name, Jervis glowered, sitting in his saddle, with his thoughts obviously miles away. Gillman certainly seemed the right name to rub Jervis up the wrong way.

'Some day I'll tell yuh a story about Gillman,' Jervis ground out harshly.

'Why not now?'

But Jervis Manley only laughed more harshly.

That night Dave Markham was in town buying several purchases for the ranch. He had a list, and as they made a goodly total they would be sent for.

He called in at the Last Chance Saloon and ordered a drink. He looked around, noted Thatch Gillman at the other end of the long bar. The ex-rancher was in dirty checkered shirt and faded dungarees rolled up over cowman's boots.

Gillman was still wearing his Colt in the little-used holster. Despite all the tales, two-gun men were not so numerous in these parts.

But maybe Gillman's favourite weapon was a rifle!

Thatch Gillman was not sober. His dark eyes gleamed out under bushy eyebrows when he saw Dave Markham. But he made no movement.

Dave had another drink, nodded to several old-timers he had known in the past and then walked to the batwing doors. He had to pass Gillman. He stopped a pace from the other man and said softly:

'Guy tried to give me a free ticket to Boothill last night. With a rifle. Just like the galoot who bush-whacked me. If yuh ever hear any tales of this varmint, yuh might like tuh pass them on, Gillman.'

The other hardly moved. His back was still towards Dave. He stared hard at his drink. His hand was nowhere near his Colt. 'I ain't heard no tales, Markham.'

'Guess it's early yet,' drawled Dave. 'Yuh can pass the word I got a bullet for the *hombre.*'

It was late that night when Dave was taking a short cut across Double J range on his way home to his own spread. There was plenty of moonlight. The land lay quiet around him with the rough lift-ing of the foothills visible nearby.

He reined his gelding when the unmistakable sound of running cattle came to his ears on the night air.

At such a late hour there could be only one

explanation for that sound. A night rider. It seemed that night riders were at Jervis Manley's Double J cattle.

Dave tapped with his spurs, sent the gelding at a hard gallop across the moonlit ground. At a gallop, it was treacherous footing. But the gelding was a great horse, and Dave trusted to its instincts.

He heard the sound of the running cattle again, and this time nearer. Then he rounded a shoulder of a wooded hill and reined in, seeing the stolen herd flowing by. The moonlight glinted on clinking, tossing horns, and there was the smell of lifted dust. Dave counted two hundred head quickly, and the outlines of a handful of night riders pushing them hard for the broken draws that led into the foothill country.

Watching the shapes of the riders in the night, he wished he had a rifle. He stood in the shade of the wood. He cursed. With a rifle even at such long range, he would have a chance of emptying a few of those saddles, but with a six-gun there was not much chance.

A Colt just didn't have the range. You had to see the whites of a guy's eyes before banking on a Colt slug finding a target. But there was a chance of getting within shooting distance. Timber swept down from the hill in a long finger to a point in the broken ground where the cattle would have to pass. It was a good chance. Dave jabbed the spurs at the bronc, went down under the shady trees.

He came out on flatter ground, still in the fringe of timber. He reined in again. Cattle hoof-beats shook the earth. He saw the first rider as cattle surged by in acrid dust. He lifted his gun from its holster, and went out into the moonlight. They would see him, but first the rustlers would hear his gun.

Crack!

He got over the first shot, his Colt flaring red flame through the night. He knew the bullet had hit when a yell of pain shot out. Startled yells came from the throats of the other night riders.

Cattle bawled in fear as other guns cracked. Dave fired back coolly into the flaming teeth of those weapons. He held the gelding firmly as it shied. His Colt bucked against his palm, and he saw one of those night riders fall in a heap from his horse.

Dave reckoned there were three furious guns against him. He had to fall back into the darkness of the wood.

The night riders came rushing straight at him. They shoved their broncs through the frightened cattle, now milling in disorder. A steel-jacketed shell screamed past Dave's ear – someone was using a saddle gun. A voice bawled:

'Get him, damn yuh! We ain't gonna let one man stop us!' Dave fired at the speaker. He thought he missed, but the voice was silent after that. And the rustlers fell back.

Dave was hidden in the shadow of the trees, and although his position was bad enough, outnumbered as he was, the night riders hesitated to rush him. Tough *hombres* they might be, but they seemed to like a whole skin.

Dave's last shots had emptied the six-gun. He took precious seconds to jack out the empty shells and load the gun again from his cartridge belt.

As he was loading a new rush of hoof-beats sounded through the night. They came from back of the rustlers and the scattered herd. Dave jerked his head. He saw a clump of half a dozen riders sweeping in to the battle. He saw the flash of their guns as they sighted the rustlers.

It could only be the Double J hands, thought Dave.

They certainly put a scare into the night riders. The rustlers whirled their horses to meet this new threat, and, sensing the real danger, they tried to scare up speed to get away from the new gun-slinging cowboys.

A saddle gun, held by one of the incoming bunch, loosened an accurate bullet and one of the rustlers dropped from his bronc. The other night riders did not wait much longer. They were giving their mounts a taste of steel spur. They had forgotten all about the herd of Double J cattle and the man who had first attacked them. They were ramming on all speed to get away from there.

Dave got the last shell into his gun and pounded

his gelding out of the trees after the fleeing rustlers. A bawling steer nearly crashed into him. Dave saw the black brand of the Double J on the animal's flank. Then he straightened his bronc again and was once more pounding after the fleeing men. On, on he went, down the throat of the gulch.

The rustling episode had been broken by Dave and then the arrival of the Double J hands. Evidently Jervis Manley's accusations of rustling in the valley had plenty of fact behind them. Who had hired the night-riders?

The fleeing men would make good their escape in the dark unless someone stopped them. Dave spurred hard, reckoning he could do that job. He hated rustlers, whether it was his own cattle that were being filched or another rancher's.

He pounded after the men, letting the Double J riders take care of the scattered cattle and the dead or dying night riders. But more guns were flashing back there and he realised they were shooting at him. It seemed they thought he was another rustler. But the bullets whizzed by; the range was too far. He was too far ahead for night shooting to be effective. With every yard he was gaining a great deal more distance. He gave no thought to the error of the Double J riders.

He had left Jervis Manley's crew and the bawling herd far behind him now. All he could hear was the pound of his bronc's hoofs, the ripple of muscle near the horse's shoulders. The rustlers were lost to view, even though the ground was moonbright. They had disappeared into the twisting narrow gulch. He rode blind into a stony gully, and headed up into the shadowy mass of the foothills.

Finally the way became pretty steep, so much that the gelding was reduced to a walk. Loose shale clattered under its hoofs. Then at the top of the ravine, Dave halted. He heard no sound that would tell him which way the night riders had gone. There was nothing in the wind. No sound came from the tangled hills stretching out for limitless miles. He let the gelding blow for a second, realising he had lost his men.

He did not know these hills sufficiently well enough to attempt a tracking, and anyway it was too dark. Regretfully he turned the bronc and headed back down the trail.

At least the rustling attempt had been broken. He wondered who was the son of a gun. Maybe it was this Slick Sadman who had operated in the valley.

Dave was closer to his own ranch than to the Double J, so he sent the tired gelding down the trail to the Lazy Cloverleaf. He could get over to see Jervis and Frank Manley in the morning. In the meantime he would hit the hay, rustlers or none!

Ned Brant had taken on the duties of general

hand, and he made a presentable breakfast next morning. Dave told him about the rustling attempt. He had decided he liked the old drifter. Better to let the old *hombre* know everything.

While Ned cleaned up the ranch-house, Dave looked round with a critical eye.

'Think I'll get myself a good carpenter from Pine City to put some more windows in this place. And what about some curtains? Didn't Gillman have any use for curtains?'

'Aw, that's woman's stuff. Yuh thinkin' o' having a woman come here, Mister Markham?'

Dave reddened. 'Maybe. Maybe.'

He promised himself to start with some paint work as soon as the material arrived from the store in Pine City.

He was in the corral putting some gear on the gelding when Jervis Manley rode into the Cloverleaf yard. He was alone. Jervis had a look of grimness on his lean, bronzed face. He climbed down from his bronc, went over to Dave's fine gelding in silence. Jervis picked up the rear hoof of the gelding and looked hard at the shoe. Then he straightened up and stared at Dave.

'Yuh got a broken shoe on that bronc. Yuh ought to get it fixed. I noticed the sign it made in the dirt the other day at my spread.'

'What are yuh getting at, Jervis?'

'Just this. Yuh were ridin' that bronc on Double J range last night, helping some other rannies shove some of my cattle into the foothills.'

Dave threw back his head and laughed.

'Are yuh loco, Jervis? Don't yuh know I was shooting at those night riders? Sure I was on Double J range last night. I was returning from Pine City. Been having a drink or two with some old pals.'

'Could it have been Gillman?' Jervis was red with fury. 'Are yuh aiming to take up where Gillman left off?'

'I tell yuh I was trading lead with those rustlers.'

Jervis Manley halted, jaw thrust forward. His whole attitude was one of distrust.

'Some galoot is trying to ruin the Double J.'

'For the last time, Jervis, I have never attempted to touch your range or your cattle, and I have no intention of doing so.'

'Guess I'll have to take yuh word,' muttered Jervis.

'Sure will. I guess it's no use asking for an apology. Yuh're sure like a bear with a sore head, Jervis. Something has yuh worried. Howabout putting the blame on this galoot Slick Sadman. I hear he took some of Charlie Kennedy's Happy S stock – long afore I hit the valley, I'm glad to tell yuh.'

'Could be,' muttered Jervis as he climbed to the saddle. 'Could be.'

He rode off, and Dave watched him with a grim smile. Jervis Manley was as suspicious as an old wolf. Something mighty queer was rodding the guy. Why did he leap to such suspicious conclusions on such flimsy evidence?

The more Dave thought about it, the more he was certain – Jervis was pretty mean because he had some secret.

About this time a rider came into a camp in the foothills. The rider was a tough waddy, and he had come out from Pine City. He had some news for his boss, Slick Sadman. And this was Slick Sadman's camp.

The rider jigged his bronc past two guards posted on rocky knolls and came to Slick Sadman.

The boss was lolling on the grass, with his head resting against an ornamental Mexican saddle. He was picking his teeth. He was a long, lean ruffian in cowboy's range clothes. He had the brand of the owlhoot trail stamped all over him. And the gang that followed him and his luck were of the same ruffian border breed.

'It was that damned tinhorn, boss,' said the rider, dropping to the ground. 'He busted the show last night. I guess he brought those Double J waddies down on us.'

'Dave Markham, huh?' scowled Slick Sadman. 'Yuh sure?'

'Gillman said so. Seems Jervis Manley bin over tuh see Dave Markham. Gillman has bin talking to a Double J waddy.'

Slick Sadman thought awhile. He was conscious

that his followers expected him to deal effectively with an enemy. If he did not act decisively, his gang would begin to doubt his leadership. On such things did his authority depend. 'That rannigan lost us that herd last night – close on two hundred head. And two men. He was shooting plenty damned straight. . . . Must be a gunslinging *hombre*. But we'll get him.'

'How yuh going to do it?'

Slick Sadman rose to his feet. He was a slouching man of six feet.

'We'll get him. Isaac here will hold the gun . . . and I'll get Markham in front of it. We'll lay a trap.'

'Yuh say he's a gunslinger,' the man named Isaac pointed out. 'I don't want to take any chances with him.'

'Don't worry about that. We'll lay this trap for him at the Last Chance. He'll be in there to-night.'

'What if he isn't?'

'But I say he will. I've got it all figured out.'

And Slick Sadman smiled thoughtfully over the sun-shimmering gulch and at the guards lolling on the rocky shoulders, cigarettes in mouths.

He knew he had to attempt something on Dave Markham as a matter of prestige. He had heard about Gillman's attempt to bushwhack the new rancher – and he sneered at the ex-rancher's blunders. There would be no blunders when Slick Sadman planned. Markham looked like being a nuisance.

THREE

BULLETS FOR BUSHWHACKERS

Ned Brant came out of the cookshack with an assortment of pans and slops. He emptied a few pans, hung them up on a nail. He went inside the cookshack, and came out again a few minutes later without his apron. He had a battered old Stetson pulled down over his bald old skull.

He came to the corral where Dave Markham was rubbing down the gelding.

'What now, boss? There's sure plenty to do round this ranch.'

Dave finished tightening a saddle belt.

'We're going tracking.'

'Huh? With all this work to do?'

'Yeah. The work can wait for a few hours. I've

got a trail to follow, and I may need help. Want to know more about those rustlers. Some people got the idea I'm mixed up with them.'

'Wal, how the heck's that?'

He smiled, but did not explain to the old waddy. But he did say a few words.

'Yeah, I want to get me some proof. I don't like being an object o' suspicion. I want to pick up the trail of those night riders who got away from me last night. Yuh willin' to come?'

'Sure.'

'Yuh any good at trackin?'

'Reckon I'm as good as an Injun scout!' cackled Ned Brant.

'There may be gunplay – if we ketch up,' warned Dave. 'I guess I didn't hire yuh for gunplay.'

Ned grinned.

'I'll get my bronc. We'll worry about gunplay when it comes.'

They rode up into the rough foothills, and then into the continually rising rocky ground. It was a cold trail by now, but Ned Brant demonstrated that he was as good as an Indian scout.He was darned good at reading trail sign. Dave, too, was no slouch, and so they made good progress along the trail. Dave kept an eye open for other strange riders. He did not want to be ambushed by the rustlers. And he did not want to bump into any of Jervis Manley's Double J riders. He wanted to investigate first.

They came to the place where Dave had lost his quarry last night. Between them they quickly discovered where he had overshot the mark.

'It was easy to miss in the dark,' said Dave. 'See this clear print of an iron shoe? Here's another, right in the gully bank. They headed out of the gulch, right up to that knife edge.'

'Yuh goin' tuh foller?'

'Sure. Like I said. I'm just plumb curious.'

The ridge brought them up to the side of a hill. Ned averred that the rustlers had cut down the ravine between the ridge and the hill. Here Ned Brant's eye was better than Dave Markham's. To Dave there was nothing to be seen but rocky shale. So Dave gave the oldster the lead.

Dave could not make anything of the trail down the ravine, and so he followed. They went on like that for another two hours, while the sun climbed higher. Once or twice Ned was hard pressed to follow sign, and Dave could not help him out. Dave would sit in the saddle patiently, rolling a cigarette, while the old drifter circled back and forward, cutting for sign. Sometimes Ned would swing down from the saddle to take a closer look at some suspicious cut in the hard earth.

It was touch and go whether the trail petered out. But between them they progressed, and they were never totally stopped for long. As the sun mounted and the morning became hotter, the two men moved slowly but steadily through the ravine, down the left of a twin canyon, across shale-covered ground and pine-needled valley. At last they came down a slope to where a stream splashed its way across a gravel bed, glinting in the sun.

Dave drew rein.

'This sure ain't hard to read!'

Cattle by the hundred had crossed that stream. There were old tracks and new. Many head had been that way before. The prints were plain in the mud. There was torn earth stretching up from the crossing, showing a much used trail.

'All right, Ned. Yuh can go back from here. Yuh got your rights. Yuh weren't hired for gunplay.'

But Ned did not turn his horse.

'Cain't see why anyone should drive stock up here,' he said. He stared hard at Dave. 'An' I don't mind burning powder in a good cause. Yuh think I should be back at the ranch putting new poles in that corral?'

But Dave just laughed quietly. 'Let's go.'

With such an obvious trail to follow, they could speed up a little, but it was a good idea to be wary. Rustlers often had lookouts posted along the way. Dave and Ned rode forward with this point in mind. The hills grew taller, steep with plenty of timber, with the sun right overhead. They could not see more than a few hundred yards because of the timber.

Ned reined in. The horses were breathing hard.

The oldster spoke suddenly.

'I can smell 'em! Cattle.'

Dave was the one to make decisions.

'Yuh sure got a nose for cattle, Ned. Maybe they're just behind that hill. We'll cut across.'

They spurred their horses against the timbered ridge. Below, at the bottom, the tracks of stolen cattle twisted out of sight. It was big, vast country. There was an immenseness about it that only those who had ridden across it for days could understand.

Half-way up the steeply pitched hill, with its covering of powdery soil and pine needles, the going became too much for the horses. They left them, tethered. Through clinging scrub they fought their way to the crest of the hill. Panting, they subsided to a fallen pine and peered down again at the scene which lay before their eyes.

They were looking down into a huge hill-enclosed pocket of mountain meadow. Evidently there was water and thick, rank grass.

Dave said under his breath: 'Jest look at all those cows. The place is pretty full!'

The patchy brown and white cows filled the meadow with pattern against the rank grass.

'Maybe four hundred head,' muttered Ned Brant.

'If I had only enough sense to bring me a glass, I might be able tuh see those brands,' fretted Dave.

He was surprised when Ned silently handed him an old battered affair. It was old but the lenses

43

were good.

The old-timer seemed to be one of those men who were always able to produce all sorts of odds and ends. Probably Ned was accustomed to carrying most of his worldly possessions around with him all the time. Most old drifters were like that – they had to be. Dave put the glass to his eye, and adjusted it. It worked, and it brought the grazing steers into sharp focus. Dave's face grew grim as he scanned one steer after another, swinging the glass across the herd as he studied the brands. Then he handed the glass back to Ned.

'Take a look, old-timer. These rustlers got Double J cattle and Happy S beef, but I can't see any Lazy Cloverleaf brands. Can yuh?'

Ned spent some time with the glass. Then: 'Ain't no Cloverleaf brands that I can see. Anyway, all yuh bought was that hundred head off Gillman – so yuh told me.'

'That's right. That's all I want, but I kinda think it mighty queer not tuh see a Cloverleaf brand. If this rustler was lifting from all the spreads in the valley, yuh'd think he'd sure get hold of some Cloverleaf stock.'

'Maybe the gang sold all the Cloverleaf beef. Sure must be a trail out o' this meadow, an' maybe some rail construction crew not far off who'ud be glad to buy beef an' no questions asked!'

'Must have some market for rustled cattle,' agreed Dave. 'Wal, this is the answer to Jervis

Manley's complaint o' missing stock. Only I kinda think it queer not to see some of Gillman's cows here.'

'Might easily bin that hundred head o' yourn here, come to think of it,' said Ned. 'They was in the foothills when we found 'em, and some galoot had driven 'em there. Maybe some other *hombres* aimed tuh pick 'em up from there.'

Dave nodded.

'I thought that way myself. And now I got an idea who that snakeroo might be.'

But he did not tell the old-timer. He thought it better to keep mere suspicions to himself.

'This sure is that Slick Sadman's hideout,' stated Ned Brant.

Dave was using the glass again.

'I see a little lean-to at the foot of the hill. It's kinda well hidden, but nature doesn't provide chimneys. No sign of any men, but I guess there must be someone to look after this cattle. If yuh—'

'Spit it out, boss,' said Ned calmly. 'If yuh want to sneak down, let's go!'

The hill was so steep and the soil so soft that they could descend simply by digging in their heels. But they went slowly, sticking to the cover of trees. They tried to avoid starting a slide of soil that would give warning to anyone below. But there was no sign of anyone as yet.

Then the small scrub cleared, and as they came into an opening there was the crack of a six-gun. A slug drilled a tree two yards from Dave's body. He thought that pretty good shooting for a sixgun, even as he dived for cover.

Ned Brant joined him. They just dropped behind a fallen pine tree. They crouched there, watching the foot of the hill.

Dave pointed to a large slab of rock on the flat.

'The shot came from there,' he said. 'Pretty good shooting.'

Ned Brant studied the scene.

'They bin laying for us. Reckon the galoot might ha' seen some soil come down the slope. But he sure got over anxious – he should ha' waited till we got into closer range. Yes, sir!'

Dave and Ned had brought their saddle guns with them in their climb up the hill, and now Dave rested the rifle muzzle across the fallen log and triggered a shot downhill at the slab of rock. Rock dust whipped from the boulder. A second later a head appeared from behind the boulder, and a hand holding a six-gun. The gun bellowed again, and lead kicked dirt a few yards short of the two men behind the log on the hill. Then the man disappeared behind the rock again.

'Seems like he ain't got no rifle,' cracked Ned Brant.

But Dave saw movement behind the rock . . . shadows. . . .

'There's two of them,' he stated.

Silence fell over the hills as the last echoes of the

46

shots faded away among the uplands. In the meadow, the cattle were stirring uneasily. A silence fell and the herd settled again. Behind the log and the rock the contestants were waiting. Dave found himself thinking:

'They've got us pinned here. But I can't say I aim tuh stay here until dark.'

It was momentarily an impasse. Ned swore, changing his cramped legs behind the log. More than once the oldster sighted his rifle on the log, but there was no real target.

And then movement.

Impatience must have been rowelling the pair behind the rock, for suddenly one of them leaped back to a dry gully that chopped the earth a few yards behind the boulder.

Dave brought his rifle up and pulled trigger, but his lead hit dust as the man fell into the concealing gully.

But Dave had seen the man clearly and recognised him. It was undoubtedly Thatch Gillman!

And then Gillman was running along the gully at a doubled crouch. Only occasionally was his head visible. Ned was secking a bead on the bobbing figure, but the other man behind the boulder emptied his gun upslope.

So Gillman was working with the rustlers! It was just as Dave suspected.

At the moment Gillman was dodging towards the lean-to, still in the almost all-concealing gully.

His pal was trying to give him cover. Undoubtedly Gillman was off to get hold of rifles.

'I'll stop that!' swore Dave.

The lean-to was out of sight from them at this point. Scrub timber swept down the hill in an unbroken curve.

'Give that hellion a few rounds, Ned.'

As Ned loosened off, Dave went moving crab-wise behind the log and then, on his feet, he ran for the shelter of the scrub timber. He reached it and went down-slope under the thick stuff. He slid and floundered in the thick soil, but he kept his hold on his rifle, determined to reach that lean-to before Gillman brought a rifle into the fight. He recalled Gillman was particularly handy with a rifle. The other hellion must have fired the first six-gun shot, for it had been pretty close.

Gillman had gained the lean-to now, and as Dave steadied in the loose soil, the other man came out now with the weapon. Dave stood behind a pine and whipped rifle to shoulder. He unleashed a bullet that smacked into the lean-to. The shot sent Gillman ducking back inside the cover. A slug came from the other man behind the boulder, but it had been fired hastily and missed Dave.

Dave was on his way again, coming down with a rush to the lean-to. If he could keep Gillman pinned in the shack, the other man might be dealt with. There were no windows in the shack. As Dave approached in a few seconds, he darted for a blind rear corner. The man behind the boulder missed with another shot. Ned's rifle barked again. Dave was now safe behind the lean-to. He paused, panting a little.

Beyond the thin wall of the lean-to he could hear the man moving around. Dave's hands tightened on the rifle. It was Gillman who had tried to kill him and steal the deed to the Lazy Clover leaf range. Indeed Gillman had tried twice. Dave had a premonition that this time would mean showdown.

There came a shout from the man still behind the rock, warning Gillman of Dave. Movement inside the lean-to ceased. Dave's jaw muscles tightened. It was a cat-and-mouse game, and it had to come to an end.

Dave crept to a corner and halted, listening for the merest sound. He braced himself, ready for a dash to the entrance and the all-important first shot.

And then he heard the snapping of a twig behind him!

He spun round, even as he realised Gillman had crept round the lean-to behind him by some miracle of stealth. He saw the other's harsh, dirty features and the rifle braced against the other's hip for a shot.

Dave's finger curled even as the other weapon flamed. The two shots mingled in one. Dave felt a bullet tug at his sleeve – and that was all.

But pain washed across Thatch Gillman's big face, and he thudded against the lean-to. The flimsy shack shook and shuddered as Gillman crumpled and hit the earth.

Dave knew the man was dead.

But he turned him over, saw the bloodstain above the heart, and knew there was nothing to do for Thatch Gillman.

FOUR

SALOON SET-TO

For a moment he was dismayed at having had to kill this man, but it had been self defence. He looked at the dead face, and then went methodically through the man's pockets, seeking for something to connect Gillman with the rustling mob. But there was nothing incriminating.

Dave got to his feet just as he heard someone on the run. He wheeled and faced Ned Brant. Ned asked: 'Is he dead?' When Dave nodded, the oldster spat. 'So's the other one. He was taking shots at yuh, an' he exposed himself once too offen. I got him.'

'There doesn't seem to be any others round here,' said Dave.

'Nope. So Gillman was running with a rustling mob?'

51

'Sure. And he was the hellion who tried to drive the hundred head of Cloverleaf cattle up to the foothills – ready for someone else to take over, I guess, only that someone didn't appear. How long did yuh work for Gillman, Ned?'

'Nary more'n a month. Never had much to do except repair fences. Reckon I was jest employed to tidy the place up while Gillman got himself a buyer.'

'I was wondering if yuh knew anything about this *hombre's* connection with these darn rustlers.'

'Never knew a durned thing.'

Dave went round to look at the other dead man. He found a hard-bitten rannigan who was a total stranger. Dave stood thinking.

'Seems to me this *hombre* was the guard here, and Gillman must ha' been on a visit – why we may never know. But I tell yuh what I want yuh to do, Ned. Stay up here awhile, and keep a peeper open durn wide. If some of the other rustlers show up see what yuh can find, but skip out if it gets too hot. I'm going down to the valley to Pine City to turn these two over to the sheriff.'

It was a plenty hard task, but Dave meant to bring down the evidence to Pine City. Ned helped him find the horses and load one with the two dead men. Then Dave said adios to Ned and rode out along the track made by the incoming cattle.

Dave made Pine City by late afternoon, and he felt real hungry. He dumped the bodies unceremoniously in the sheriff's jail, while the sheriff stood and scowled. He listened to Dave's story.

'Only gang o' rustlers round these parts be Slick Sadman's outfit,' grunted the sheriff. 'Guess I'll get myself a posse and take a look at those rustled cattle.'

'Wal, yuh can see for yourself this is the end o' Thatch Gillman,' drawled Dave.

The gnawing emptiness in Dave's stomach was very real. It was near sunset, and he had had nothing to eat all day. He went along to an eating-house, had some supper.

He came out feeling a lot better. Along the dusty main stem of Pine City he saw the painted false front of the Last Chance Saloon. Dave hesitated. It was early in the evening, and he was not a hard drinking man. But like any other cowboy in the rough Western towns, he saw no reason to be an abstainer.

He wandered along the boardwalk, turned into the batwing doors of the Last Chance. The familiar clink of gold coins came to his ears as gamblers sat at corner tables. Oil lamps were lit, and the counter wet with drink rings. The place was crowded with men, lean riders who knew the territory backwards, better-dressed ranchers, cowboys in from roundup and eager for the rye.

Dave ran an eye over the company, guessed there were at least three dozen men, booted, spurred and gun-wearers. There was a rattle of glasses, the hubbub of conversation, white-coated bartenders with waxed moustaches.

He ordered his drink, and leaned his elbows on the mahogany counter. Dave felt conscious of the dirt on his levis overalls tucked into his boots. He felt he ought to get home and change into a bright red shirt, brown and tan trousers tucked into shiny riding boots. Then, maybe, go along and see Mabel North. He felt he ought to talk to the girl. Maybe he should tell Jervis Manley that Gillman was dead. Jervis would be glad to hear that news, he felt.

But maybe the news had spread already. Folks had seen him bringing the dead men into town.

Yeah, it would be a good idea to ride over to the Double J. If he did not see Jervis, he would see Mabel.

He was about to finish his drink and turn round when he saw the figure of Jervis Manley in the long ornamental mirror at the back of the bar. Dave turned casually, grinned at Jervis. His boyhood friend came up, hesitated for a second, then shot out his hand. 'I heard yuh killed Gillman. Shake, Dave. I'm sorry for anything rotten I said to yuh. Yuh killed a snake.'

'It was self-defence. I've seen the sheriff, reported the shooting to him.'

'Yeah, the news got out to me mighty quick. I said I could tell yuh a story about Gillman one day – well, I don't know. With him dead, I oughta let things lie. But what I am goin' to tell yuh will lower me in your estimation, Dave. To cut out the fancy talk, I will tell yuh Gillman an' me did some crooked brand work with some cattle that didn't belong to either of us.

'I was in a tough spot at the time – the drought was hangin' on, some of my beef were not strong enough to trail-herd to the markets. So I went in with Gillman. He was crooked and vicious as a coyote. In the end he began to blackmail me. He double-crossed me right and left. I figure I was a pretty poor sort of mug to a varmint like him. Many times I just itched for an excuse to shoot it out with him, but the skunk never gave me the chance. Wal, he's dead now, and I'm mighty glad.'

'Yuh don't need to say any more, Jervis,' interrupted Dave. 'I guessed yuh had worries. Gillman rustled your cattle. Yuh'll find plenty Double J cows in that upland meadow. I reckon Slick Sadman used Gillman plenty often.'

'Time that hellion was cleared from the valley – and the foothills!' snapped Jervis. 'I think we oughta get together – you, me and Charlie Kennedy of the Happy S.'

'Any time yuh like to get a posse together,' drawled Dave. 'I could get my other six-gun out o' cold storage.'

'Yeah, yuh'd need two guns with them polecats,' growled Jervis.

'Have a drink,' invited Dave.

He had them ordered and the glasses were on the counter. Dave raised the glass to his lips to down it and his eyes flicked over at the ornamental mirror. He saw six men push through the batwing doors with a get-to-hell-outa-my-way attitude. A hush fell over the saloon. Dave lowered his drink as someone breathed, 'Slick Sadman's outfit!'

The clink of coins had ceased. Men had stiffened where they sat or stood. Then, as the six men walked up to the bar, men began to move quietly towards the doors. They were men who reckoned they had no quarrel with the rustler outlaw, and saw no reason why they should get in the way of lead trouble.

It was a pretty bold move of Slick Sadman's. Pine City had not seen his like for a long time. The town boasted prosperity and peace. Gun-fights were not too frequent. Trouble could be found in the foothills where men argued over cattle and brands, but the town was governed by law-abiding men.

By his very audacity Slick Sadman had barged into the Last Chance without opposition.

Dave wondered what the rustler wanted. He soon found out.

'Thought we'd find yuh here, Markham,' drawled Slick Sadman. 'We sent a waddy with some news to the Double J to rowel Jervis Manley into seeking yuh. We thought yuh'd end up in the saloon. Celebratin', huh?'

Slowly, Dave turned his back to the counter, faced the border ruffian. Jervis casually moved with him. Both men had their thumbs stuck in the belts – hands sufficiently near to their one six-gun, but not too near to provoke premature trouble. But trouble was pretty plain on the horizon.

Dave studied the rustler. He saw a lean, hatchet-faced half-Mexican with two six-guns. He wore a sombrero with a knotted leather thong below his unshaven chin. He had black wicked eyes. But there was a cunning gleam in those eyes. It would not pay anyone to underestimate a *hombre* of this kind.

'Celebratin'? Reckon I don't understand, stranger.'

The bartender had reluctantly placed drinks before the men. Slick Sadman's chief side-kick had merely jerked a dirty bullet-shaped head to denote the order. The party had split into two. On Dave's side was Slick Sadman and two men, and on Jervis Manley's side were the other three. They were all lean, border ruffians of the owl-hoot trail. They were tall and short, scrubby and unshaven. They leaned against the bar with one elbow so that they could survey a wide arc of the saloon. They were hard-bitten rannies, but they valued their skin same as any other *hombre*. The man who threw his hand for holster would invite trouble. It seemed no one in the saloon wanted trouble.

'Ain't yuh celebratin' yuh first kills in the valley?'

drawled Slick Sadman.

'Not particularly.'

Dave was non-committal. He had to play this hellion along, and be ready for trouble at the same time.

The rustler's eyes gleamed.

'Maybe we made a mistake. Maybe it wasn't yuh and another stinkin' polecat who shot Gillman and Metz.'

'I shot Gillman,' said Dave deliberately. 'An' my pardner shot the other *hombre*. It was a fair fight. Yuh think it wasn't?'

'We think it was murder!' hissed Slick Sadman.

Dave smiled.

'Yuh entitled to yuh opinion, pal.'

Slick Sadman narrowed his eyes. He was simply playing for the slightest excuse to start throwing lead. So far he had not rowelled Dave into giving him that excuse.

One of the border outfit had moved over to the batwing doors with his rye. He had stared out into the oil-lighted street, across the dusty road and the boardwalk and tie-rails.

He flung words to his chief.

'Thet old sheriff is on his way, Slick. With his deputy. Coming along the boardwalk, the old tin-badge!'

Slick Sadman grinned.

'That *hombre* has never thrown a gun for two years.' He swung again to Dave. He said insolently:

58

'Yuh crossed my trail, Mister Markham. I don't think I like yuh ornery face!'

It was meant as a challenge and insult. Dave accepted it with a lightning swiftness that matched Slick Sadman's.

But not the way Slick Sadman wanted it.

Dave saw in a flash that there was trickery. Slick Sadman was not offering to shoot it out with his own worthy body as a possible target. Dave had seen, just as the rustler chief spoke his challenge, a movement on the part of the man next to Slick Sadman.

It was only the merest tensing of the man's general attitude. But Dave, out of long experience of tricksters, guessed what was coming.

Slick Sadman planned murder, not a straight-forward shooting! Dave's hand hit leather and whipped up. His .45 spat flame with a roar – and the slug hurtled at the man next to Slick Sadman. It slugged in deep and the man crumbled with a silly look on his face. The partly-moved gun in his holster fell out of its own accord. Dave's gun slashed in an arc and belched flame at Slick Sadman as the outlaw moved his gunhand with a speed that matched Dave's . . . or almost matched Dave's.

The bullet from the young rancher's gun bit into his arm with paralysing force, causing the outlaw to drop his six-gun as if it suddenly weighed a ton. He backed with the force of the biting slug.

He gripped his arm and swore.

Slick Sadman had planned to draw on Dave, no doubt, with his side-kick contributing the bullet which would kill because it would be unleashed a second before any proper move had been made.

The trick had not come off.

'Over the counter, Jervis!' Dave shouted as bedlam let loose. Seconds only had elapsed. The two incredibly speedy shots . . . and then the fall of a body . . . Slick Sadman staggering back . . . then the two ranchers leaping over the bar counter . . . all in a few seconds.

But shots detonated quickly in the next ten seconds. Men scrambled to cover, to the doors. Slick Sadman's outfit backed to the walls, unleashing a fusillade of shots at the counter. Bits of mahogany splintered in all directions. Dave and Jervis together with a gulping bartender waited until the first fusillade had expended itself. Dave judged the outlaws would have to spend at least a few seconds in reloading.

His arm came up, over the counter, and his finger triggered three shots at random into the wall. Jervis followed suit. Their chance bullets evidently found a target, for one rustler bawled in rage and pain.

Then Dave peered through the acrid cloud of powder smoke and aimed at one rustler. The man jerked convulsively as the bullet hit his stomach. Dave triggered for another but missed as he instinctively flinched at an exploding gun in the saloon. Jervis had followed Dave's example and was peering over the bar counter, aiming steadily. Guns lanced flame. The saloon was empty of customers. Then Jervis stumbled against Dave and folded up behind the counter. His collapse was only temporary, however, for he staggered to his feet again, clutching his shoulder, his six-gun still in his hand.

A number of shots spat out from the darkness just outside the batwing doors. The shots were aimed at the rustler gang, though rather wildly.

'Let's git!' bawled one man. 'Thet durned sheriff and his deputy is out thar.'

There was a general movement of the rustlers to the batwing doors. They went shooting as they moved, making a veritable inferno of noise. They were wild bullets, but random slugs had a queer habit of finding a target. No one stood around when bullets whined. Most folks ducked.

Two rustlers would not ride again. One was the man who had tried to get the drop on Dave, and the other had been killed by Dave in the battle.

The saloon was badly chipped. The mirror was broken, and glass had fallen to the ground. Brass cartridge shells lay around. Slick Sadman's outfit got out quickly, jumped their horses and spurred down the dusty street. One or two citizens fired a Colt at them, but hitting a speeding horseman in the night was always a gamble.

Dave stood on the boardwalk and emptied his gun again. But the frantically spurring horsemen got away.

He went back to see Jervis Manley.

'Only a shoulder wound,' said Jervis. 'Those pack rats wanted to get yuh, Dave. Wonder to me why they didn't. I admit I was scared.'

Dave grinned as he looked expertly at the other's wound. 'Sure. So was I. I'm always scared before a fight. It's a hell of a feeling!'

Jervis went over and stirred the fallen gunman with his foot. 'Yuh sure caught on to that *hombre's* play quick, Dave,' he said admiringly. 'If it had been me, he'd ha' got me before I tumbled.'

'Wal, Jervis, I figured something queer was on the moment the six men came in. If Slick Sadman wanted to get me personally he could have faced me alone. No, those *hombres* were all part of a cover-up. And this rannigan here moved his shoulders too quickly. I guess it was just instinct on my part.'

'Slick Sadman must be sore at yuh busting up his play with the rustled cattle. He's a real border rat, that varmint.'

The sheriff waddled in, gun still smoking. His deputy, a younger man, looked over the two dead men.

'Two o' 'em, huh? Yuh sure were lucky to come outa that alive, Mister Markham,' said the sheriff.

'Two less, anyway,' said the deputy. 'But that owlhoot will soon line up another pair, an' he's got a camp up in the hill country somewheres.'

'Oughta get a posse an' get after them,' grunted the sheriff. 'But they'd jest outride us. They done it before.'

Customers were coming back to see the damage and the dead men. The sheriff, whose name was Tom Parson, called to some men to give him a hand with the bodies. Two more for the town jail.

'Need to git me a mortuary!' he grunted.

'I'll get back to my spread to see if Ned has turned up,' said Dave.

'I'll ride out with yuh,' grunted Jervis.

There was a bright moon as they rode over the mesquite towards the Double J and the Lazy Cloverleaf. Dave told all he knew about the cattle grazing in the upland meadow.

'Got to get them outa there,' grunted Jervis, and he wiped the back of his neck. 'With this heat browning the grass every day and the beef being in the one place, there won't be much feeding left for them after a few more days. Slick Sadman won't go near the meadow for fear of running into a posse, an' if the cows stray into them ravines, it'll be one heck of a job rounding 'em up. Wal, got to get me some sleep. Adios, Dave. Thanks for everything.'

Dave turned off the trail and rode over to his spread. He hoped Ned Brant had returned.

There was plenty of heat in the earth, he

reflected. Undoubtedly another week or two of this continuing heat would constitute a drought with all the anxieties it brought to cattle ranchers.

He found old Ned Brant sound asleep in the bunkhouse! The old-timer did not even stir as Dave looked in, smiling. Evidently the old drifter had got tired of waiting for his boss to return.

Dave copied the old-timer, but his gun lay under his pillow, and his gun-belt a foot from his head. If he wanted to buckle it on quickly, he could easily reach it. He knew he had made an enemy of Slick Sadman, and the in-bitten half-Mexican, like most of his kind, would not forget quickly.

When the next day dawned, he put in a good many hours of work around the ranch. The corral needed new posts ... Ned cleaned the ranch-house ... horses needed grooming ... fencing needed renewing.

By late afternoon they had got through a fair amount. Dave paused in his efforts, and by chance saw the dust cloud on the horizon. He studied it for a moment and decided it was made by a passing herd. It could be either Double J or Happy S cattle. The dust cloud was right among the foothills. Then he knew what it was.

'Jervis must have got that beef o' his outa that upland meadow. Maybe Charlie Kennedy is with him. Sure would like tuh see that fat old *hombre* again. Ain't clapped eyes on him since I came back to the valley!'

64

He said nothing to Ned, but saddled his gelding. He rode out with thundering hoofs over the mesa. The sun was climbing high in its arc, and soon would be overhead. Then it would be a brassy orb. Already the grass was thinning out and browning; that was only to be expected at this time of the year.

With the thinning grass came dust in the valley. But up in the hills, in the sprawling saw-toothed ranges, the magnificent ocotillo flared in scarlet streaks, and in the thin breeze salmon and orange chollas and opuntias swayed. But the mesquite covered valley held the heat. Only in the mountains and foothills was it cooler under the juniper, cedar and pine trees.

It was a good many miles across the wide valley to the arroyos and gullies of the foothills, and before the ground began to rise he encountered scrub country. Cactus and prickly pear. Clumps of sage and crisp mesquite grass. The dust cloud hung over the herd. Dave approached right up, and saw the cattle were being driven slowly down a narrow ravine which was studded with brush. Once out of the ravine they would steadily approach the plains. He saw riders – perhaps only five men. One was Jervis Manley, and another huge figure could only be the fat, jovial Charlie Kennedy. The ranchers were seeing to it personally that they got back all their rustled stock. Jervis, no doubt, would detach his cows from the herd as soon as they reached the easy-going plain.

The ravine was fringed with a crooked line of dead cedars which had been blasted by lightning at some distant date. The trees were pretty thick, with brush intermingling everywhere. The cattle were slow. They were lazy, having been well-fed during their sojourn in the upland meadow. Maybe they were reluctant to leave. Sharp-horned cattle could be ornery creatures!

Dave came up and hailed Jervis. He was glad to see the cattle had been retrieved, and it had been mainly to satisfy his curiosity that he had ridden over.

'Plumb glad to see yuh got those beefs, Jervis,' he said cordially. 'Well fed, too. Yuh oughta thank Slick Sadman. That mountain meadow gets plenty of moisture.'

'Heck of a job driving steers down this country,' grunted Jervis. 'Some ornery galoot exchanged lead with us up in them hills! Must ha' bin Slick Sadman's outfit!'

'Wal, we spoilt his play.'

The words were no sooner out of Dave's mouth when confused shouting broke out among the other punchers!

As if by magic, red flames shot up ahead of the driving herd. Right across the mouth of the ravine fire licked up among the dry brush and scrub. With incredible rapidity it spread to the dead cedars. There was a wall of flame.

Even as the flames appeared, Dave saw the two riders spurring madly across the ravine mouth. They were dragging torches of inflammable material, fastened to their saddles with a draw chain. They had fired the summer-parched brush!

Slick Sadman's men again, without a doubt!

FIVE

FIRE AND A
FEMALE

Red tongues of flame leaped skywards like pillars in an inferno. The scarlet streak moved on, racing swiftly, firing brush and sage in a wavering red line. The herd was spooked, and they lowered their heads and bawled.

On the right and on the left of the ravine the flare flitted like a powder trail through the dried grass towards another clump of dead-wood trees. A wall of flame now crackled hungrily all round the herd. The fire lines curved like prongs, blocking any escape from the ravine.

'We're trapped!' yelled one puncher. 'We'll get singed – at the best. And the cattle, too!'

Dave had drawn his gun and fired a load at the

two disappearing riders on the other side of the consuming flames. But they were a long way off, mere jerking puppets on madly spurring broncs.

Another second, as the roundup men tried to herd the cattle, and the riders disappeared into a parallel ravine.

The herd bellowed with fright. They were badly spooked. The six riders jigged their horses and closed together in a clump. There was no doubt they were surrounded by the inferno, and worse, the fire would rapidly move up and engulf them. There was plenty of dried scrub all around and under their very feet. Behind the six men the unmistakable rumble of hoofs grew worse. The cattle, frightened and dazed by the fire, were moving. The men were in front of some four hundred maddened sharp-horned steers in a narrow ravine. Before them the fire crackled menacingly. Behind them the cattle would soon move in blind terror.

'That durned rattler Sadman!' yelled Jervis Manley above the commotion. 'He aims tuh burn the hides of us an' the cattle!'

'Quick!' shouted Dave. 'Get yore horses up the ravine's sides before the fire narrows the circle. Then get round to the rear o' this herd. They'll stampede any moment now. Listen to 'em!'

Even as he spoke the maddened herd rushed into a wild, hurtling mass. They were pounding along the ravine bed towards the rim of fire.

''They'll stampede right up to the flames an' then turn!' yelled Dave. 'I sure wouldn't like tuh be under those hoofs when they try to turn all at once! Git your horses up the ravine side!'

It was a tough trick to accomplish in a matter of a few seconds. But the other horsemen tried to follow Dave's gelding. Dave had a fine horse. It knew a few tricks which were the result of hours of careful training. Moreover, the horse had spent years in picking a way across some of the most risky trails in the West.

The gelding strained and slithered with forelegs and hindlegs as it almost clawed up a steep slope. Up and up, in a series of jerks. The horsemen below followed, and the last of them just cleared the ravine floor when the first of the red-eyed, bawling steers dashed madly by.

Dave's gelding gained a rough, crumbling ridge which swept along parallel with the ravine bed, but at a height of about twelve feet. Below the steep slope the herd was charging and bawling towards the rim of red flames and hot ashes. Dave rode along the ridge, gesturing to the others to follow. Without wasting a second the horsemen rode along until the ridge dipped and led down to the ravine again.

Now they were behind the maddened herd. The cowboys peered through smoke and dust, saw the wildly tossing horned heads and heaving rumps.

'They'll turn!' yelled Dave. 'They'll push each

other into the fire. Those cows will go plumb mad when the heat bites.'

'Tarnation!' roared a puncher. 'We'll be in their path again!'

'That's not so,' shouted Dave. 'We've got to keep 'em running the way they've taken already – right through the flames. Get the whole herd barging ahead, an' they'll beat a path through. Nothin' can stop a stampeding herd. Come on!'

'Git goin', men!' bawled Jervis.

They spurred their broncs forward, drawing Colts at the same time. It was a risky task, but better than waiting until the fire swept up right under the cattle.

The horses snorted under the taste of steel spurs, but they pounded forward. Six-guns began to bark.

Crack! Crack! Crack!

The six horsemen came right up close to the heaving flanks of the last steers. They reloaded six-guns and volleyed them into the air again. The cattle, maddened before, were now absolutely uncontrollable. The steers in the rear pressed on, their weight sending the leading cows into the hot flames. Scrub, sage and mesquite were blazing furiously. Dust and red hot ashes flew into the air, churned by hundreds of pounding hoofs.

To the six men pressing against the rear cattle, it was a task fraught with danger. The men knew it, too. They knew their chances of survival amidst a stampeding herd were pretty low – if the herd turned from the fire in spite of the startling noises in the rear.

But already the leading steers were half-way through the fire belt, pressed on by the maddened cattle behind, which had yet to taste the heat, but were deadly panicked by the hulla-balloo that drove them on.

They were minutes of dangerous confusion. True the cowboys could have climbed the ravine sides and left the cattle to their fate. Some of the cattle would have emerged, scorched and crazy, but otherwise all right. But a good many would have dashed their bodies to pieces against the rocks around. They would go berserk, repeatedly trying to crash a way through hard rock.

Under Dave's plan some would be scorched, but within a minute or so would clear the fire belt.

And the plan came off! The momentum of the crazed herd was maintained, and hoofs beat a path straight through. The lead steers suffered, but those in the rear benefitted by the stamped-out trail. When the cowboys dashed through, they nearly choked with hot ash, but the actual flames had died under the pounding of cattle hoofs.

Once in the clear the cattle got into a mad stride that would expend itself on the miles of prairie valley. Six riders watched them go. The men skidded their horses to a halt, looked round at each other.

'Everyone all right?' called out huge Charlie Kennedy. He wiped sweat and ash from his face and big jowls.

'Seems like it,' said Jervis, glancing around. 'My two hands are here – and your man, I see. But where's Dave Markham? Holy smoke – did he—?'

'Thar he is!' barked one cowboy, and he pointed at the still pounding herd.

Dave was galloping his gelding at a simply amazing pace as if he had suddenly taken leave of his senses. At least, that was the way it seemed to the other five riders.

'Where in tarnation does he think he's going?' growled Charlie Kennedy. 'Sure ain't no need tuh chase thet herd. They'll tire themselves out long afore they cut up that mesa with their hoofs!' Suddenly Jervis Manley shouted in horror.

'Look! There's a rider right ahead o' that herd, by thunder! Damn! It's a girl – Mabel North! How—'

He wasted no more words, but spurred his horse into a fast gallop.

But there was nothing Jervis Manley could do. He was too far behind the herd.

Dave Markham had seen the girl rider the instant he had cleared the ravine. By chance he had stopped to follow the thundering herd's progress, and the small, lone figure riding slowly across the prairie had met his gaze.

He had sized the situation in a flash, though he

was not sure why the girl did not spur her horse the instant she saw the herd thundering towards her.

He did know, however, that she was in danger, and, instinctively, he had rowelled his gelding into a mad gallop. Without a word to the others – there was not time – he had ridden away, keeping pace with the outside steers.

In the few minutes left to him as he rode swift as death in a gun-fight, he thought he knew why Mabel North was riding alone across the mesquite. She was probably taking a leisurely ride to see the retrieved cattle coming down from the foothills.

But why did she not strive to get her horse and herself out of the path of the charging herd?

And then, as he grimly urged the gelding past the flank of the bawling, red-eyed mass of steers, he saw why the girl could not save herself.

Her pinto was lame!

Mabel was, indeed, trying to hustle the pony, but the animal could not make it. The pinto was slowed to a walk, a mere hobble. Even if Mabel tried to leave the pinto and save herself, there just would not be time. The herd would be on her, with thundering hoofs beating the life-blood from her!

But there was a chance that Dave's gelding could outstrip the cattle. The mass of beef was slowing, too. The madness was leaving them. But they would travel a long way yet before they finally slowed down.

Dave rowelled the gelding unmercifully. The horse responded, leaving the lead steers at last. More yards of mesquite grass passed beneath the gelding's pounding hoofs. The horse was wide-eyed with the effort. But it was a magnificent animal, as Dave knew. A horse among thousands, and that was why he had chosen it, trained it as he had never trained a horse before.

He was riding ten . . . twenty . . . yards ahead of the stampeding herd. He saw Mabel turn her horse, jigging the pinto along the same direction as the streaming herd. The pinto, lame though it was, might be carried along with the herd when the cows overtook it. But caught at an angle, the creature would go down. . . .

But Dave planned to sweep the girl from the pinto's back before the herd was anyway near.

She sensed his intention like the born horse-woman that she was. She was ready when the panting gelding finally galloped up. She had jigged the pinto into a little trot, and Dave had little need to check the gelding's momentum. His right arm curved out like a hook . . . he swept into her and heaved. She was lifted from the pinto's back and deposited across the gelding as if the feat were one of constant practice.

Mabel had helped Dave by her good sense and cool nerve. Even as she was hoisted through the air, she had contrived to come down on the gelding with her riding-booted legs astride the horse.

Bearing the double load, the gelding strove to gallop off at an angle to the left. For a moment the herd actually decreased the gap as the horse took the turn, but soon Dave saw they had crossed the point where every yard was an actual yard to one side of the dust-raising cattle.

He finally brought the gelding to a halt seventy-five yards on the flank of the passing herd. The horse stood snorting and blowing, still wide-eyed with the strain.

Dave patted the gelding's neck. 'Extra feed for yuh, old pal.'

Mabel sat in front of Dave, and he could feel the beating of her heart as his arms steadied her. Too, the nearness of her body was a new sensation, even after the consecutive thrills of the past events.

'We made it,' he said.

'Reckon I'd be a sight if those steers had bumped me,' she gasped.

He nodded gravely.

'I was scared stiff when I saw yuh, Mabel!' he blurted out. 'How come that pinto went lame?'

'Well, it was just one of those things. I was coming over to see Jervis bring down the cattle, and I guess I tried to gallop too fast. The pinto stepped in a jack-rabbit hole, and I nearly came off. But what was the fire?'

'Slick Sadman's galoots set fire to the brush an' tried to pin us in that ravine,' he said briefly. 'Guess they followed Jervis down from the hills.

But you – Mabel, are yuh all right?'

'Sure.' She smiled. 'I'm all right – now!'

'I'm sure glad,' he said fervently. 'Yuh sure gave me a scare. Don't ever do it again!'

'I won't, Dave.' Her voice was low. 'Let me down, Dave. I wonder if the pinto got out o' the herd safely?'

'If he did, yuh'll still need carrying,' he said.

He did not set her down. She was half-turned to him. He could smell the fragrance of her hair, and as she moved her soft cheek touched his brown, dust-laden face. It was a wonderful experience to Dave Markham – a man who had never philandered with women. In his stern, disciplined mind he carried an image of a girl who was vaguely his ideal – and the image had an astonishing likeness to Mabel North. He had had the same thoughts over the past three years, when he had been many hundreds of miles from the valley.

She, too, sensed his thoughts. 'Dave, Jervis is riding up!'

'Tell me, Mabel,' he said urgently. 'Are yuh – yuh free – in yuh heart, I mean?'

'I am not free, Dave Markham!'

She was smiling, but he did not notice, so great was his consternation.

'Yuh mean . . . Jervis . . . I heard tell . . . yuh and Jervis. . . .'

She was confused for all her little joke.

'No, Dave. Not Jervis . . . he never meant

anythin' to me. No one has except . . . except. . . .'

'Who is it?' he asked.

She was more than ever confused.

'I can't tell yuh – yuh big idiot, Dave Markham!' She slapped the gelding's side. 'Get along with yuh horse. I want to find my pinto!'

And Jervis had ridden up even as Dave realised the great, marvellous truth!

He did not see the peculiar expression on Jervis Manley's face when he saw the girl sitting close to Dave. Jervis had seen them talking earnestly, long after all danger from the cattle had gone.

For a good many months Jervis had paid a lot of attention to Mabel North, though it galled him to realise that she treated him no differently than anyone else. This he knew; he had even asked her to marry him, and she had refused. At the time of his troubles with Thatch Gillman, this refusal had added to his bitter thoughts.

Now to see Dave Markham and Mabel with their heads together roused feelings he would have liked to control, for he knew his weaknesses, but some emotions were strong. And this sight of the girl he hoped to marry one day, even if she refused him now, so obviously close to another man was more than his finer feelings could bear.

He was abrupt in his first words. 'Yuh pinto's over there, Mabel.'

'He's all right! Oh, good!'

'Yeah, he got outa that stampede as if it were a

miracle. Yuh all right, Mabel?'

'Not a scratch. Dave was wonderful. Did yuh see the way his gelding outrode that herd?'

Jervis all but scowled.

'Yeah' – grudgingly – 'reckon Dave is pretty smart.' He glanced quickly at the other man. 'Yuh did a good job, Dave. Mabel's pinto is over by that sage clump.'

It was a hint that the girl could ride her own horse.

'So I see,' drawled Dave, secretly amused. 'But yuh seem to overlook the fact that the hoss is lame, Jervis. Reckon we'll put a hitch on the pinto's saddle an' ride into the Double J. My gelding can sure take a double load at a trot any old time.'

And Jervis had to comply grudgingly. Worse for him, perhaps, and rankling in his mind no matter how he tried to shut the feeling out, was the knowledge that Mabel certainly liked Dave Markham.

One look at her face told a story. Her eyes were shining. There was something in her expression as she tucked a wisp of golden brown hair under her hat.

Then the Double J waddies rode up and asked if the cattle were to be rounded up and taken to the pasture. Their tonc implied that Jervis ought to go along and supervise the sorting of the cattle.

There might be a question of brands. Charlie Kennedy would want Jervis to be present when the cattle were sorted.

So Jervis rode off with the others and the owner of the Happy S. Dave turned his horse slowly towards the Double J spread, seen in the distance across the valley as a blur of low buildings.

There were none of his cattle among the retrieved stock, so he had nothing really to do with them.

Charlie Kennedy and Jervis ought to be grateful to him for helping to save the beef from the fire.

Slick Sadman was no doubt bent on revenge. Such an exploit could gain him no profit, but plenty of enemies. Any more such adventures, and the sheriff of Pine City would be forced to make a determined effort to clear Slick Sadman out of the hills around the valley. Folks would tolerate so much – they had to in a Western cattle and mining town where much law depended on the six-gun. But law-abiding people inevitably demanded law when bandits became too troublesome.

Dave and Mabel rode in silence for a few minutes. Both had inner thoughts, some of which they would dearly have liked to spill. But the girl obviously had to wait, and the man seemed to find difficulties.

Dave had sensed Jervis Manley's animosity. He knew exactly what was wrong. He had been slow in sensing the trouble at first, because of the glow Mabel's words had inspired inside him, but Jervis's remarks had given his thoughts away.

If he courted Mabel, Jervis would take on a

grouch just when it seemed better feelings were to be gained between them.

But Jervis could go and jump in the river!

'Mabel,' he began slowly. 'I bin away from the valley three years an' yuh haven't. I've bin away shootin' it out with badmen an' collecting bounties. Yuh understand, Mabel? I've killed a few men, an' it was mostly for money and excitement. Yuh understand, Mabel? I'm just a rough sort of *hombre* who has come home to – to sorta settle down, get my roots in some soil. I want yuh to understand, Mabel, I'm right ready tuh settle down.'

'You like the valley, Dave?'

'Sure do. This is a mighty fine country. Say, yuh haven't bin over to my spread yet. What about riding over now?'

'I'd like to, but I reckon I'd better take the pinto home first.'

'Sure. Then we could go right over.' He was enthusiastic. Jervis and his animosity were forgotten. 'I'd sure like tuh show yuh what I aim to do with that outfit pretty soon. That *hombre* Gillman just plain neglected the place. I aim tuh fix that ranch-house so most people round here will be fair amazed.'

'Yuh going to be a big rancher in the valley, Dave?'

He turned serious eyes on her.

'Yeah. I've got plans. With a bit of luck and an end to this drought, I ought to do well. Might take a year or two. Reckon if I had a – a – girl who'd like tuh help. . . .'

He broke off, afraid to go any further.

'A girl, Dave?' She turned wide blue eyes to him.

He plunged, and if his voice was hoarse, he put it down to the dust.

'Sure, Mabel. A girl like you as a wife . . . it's just an ordinary spread . . . not as big as the Double J . . . but with a girl like yuh, Mabel. Oh gosh! I'm not much good at saying this . . . Will yuh marry me, Mabel?'

She just came closer to him and looked up with appealing eyes. He reined the horse, and gripped her arms. There was now no need for words. But before he kissed her, she had time to say: 'I'll marry you, Dave, anytime.'

He kissed her fervently, and then after a moment or two she broke away with a little gasp.

'Mabel, I love yuh. I reckon I always did. I always used to think about yuh when I was away. Couldn't get yuh outa my mind altogether.'

She nestled closer. The gelding cropped at some grass.

'You're my man, Dave. I love you, too. I was always wondering when I'd see yuh again – and I didn't know why I felt that way!'

He laughed.

'Sure, we were both in love! Oh boy! What a mighty fine thing this is! Say, let's get over to that spread o' mine. We sure got some plans to make now!'

'You bet, Dave. But first I've got to take the pinto back to the ranch.'

He hustled the gelding along after that, but not too fast for the game little pinto which was hobbling along on the end of a rope. Soon they came up to the Double J ranch-yard and as Dave reined in and allowed Mabel to jump down, a man came out of the bunk-house and strode over to them. Dave looked up.

Within seconds his eyes narrowed under his sombrero. There was a steadfast purpose about the stride of this man which he did not like.

He was a big *hombre*, and Dave did not know him. But it seemed he was one of the hands around the Double J. Dave guessed the man must be one of the newcomers.

The man came right up to Dave as he sat the horse.

'I saw yuh kissing Miss North!' grated the man.

Dave stared coolly.

'Yuh did, pal? Then yuh sure saw something that wasn't intended for yuh eyes!'

His reply was straightforward because he had instantly taken a dislike to the *hombre* as well as his first words and the way he spoke them.

The man stared back with fury in his lean, leathery face and hawk-like eyes. He was dressed in range clothes – dusty boots with an old levis overall tucked into them. His shirt was black, with faded pearl buttons. He wore a six-gun low down on his thigh. He looked an in-bitten rannigan to Dave's coolly appraising glance.

'I'll teach yuh to molest a girl from the Double J!' bawled the man.

'Jest a minute, pard.' Dave leaned forward in the saddle. 'Do yuh know who I am? I worked on this ranch as a kid. I know Mabel North and Jervis and Frank. My name is Dave Markham.'

'I know yuh, *hombre*!' sneered the man. 'An' my name is Lash Logan. I'm a pal o' Jervis Manley, ef yuh want to know. An' I was a pal o' Thatch Gillman! An' I'm foreman o' this spread. And on top o' all that, Mister Markham, I got orders to throw out all ornery galoots who try to take advantage of Miss Mabel.'

Dave breathed hard, trying to retain his patience. It was difficult in front of the girl.

'So yuh got orders, huh? Whose orders?'

'The boss gave the orders,' said Lash Logan. 'Jervis sure doesn't like strange *hombres* stampin' round this ranch-yard trying to pass the time o' day with Miss Mabel.'

There was a gasp of indignation from Mabel North.

'Jervis should know I can take care of myself! I won't stand for this!'

'Do you intend to git?' challenged Lash Logan.

The foreman of the Double J was pressing the affair, Dave knew. He guessed something right away. This rannigan was a pal of the dead Gillman. Maybe he and Gillman were the same breed – it certainly seemed that way. Why Jervis had hired him as foreman passed comprehension – unless it had been done under some sort of compulsion. Jervis Manley had had trouble with Gillman, and maybe many strange plays had been made.

'I intend to take Miss North over to the Lazy Cloverleaf,' said Dave calmly. 'And in which case I shall have to wait here until she gets another horse. Maybe I'll help her saddle it, if yuh have no dislike to that little idea.'

'Why, yuh—'

Lash Logan made a play to pull Dave down from the gelding, but it was frustrated from the start.

Dave lightly leaped to the ground and backed to gain room. Lash Logan took this as a retreat and he hastened forward with a glitter of triumph in his eyes. But he stopped dead when Dave piled a right fist into his jaw. The foreman of the Double J rocked on his heels for a moment while Dave calmly waited for the man's retaliation. Had Logan dropped his aggression there and then, Dave would have been satisfied. So he waited, actually giving the man a chance to recover.

Then Lash Logan came in with weaving fists. He had a wary glint in his black eyes now. His left shot out, connected with Dave's face. Dave piled another blow at the other's hawk-like nose and saw it bleed. Then both men were fighting furiously.

The foreman had a rocky chin, but Dave had dynamite in both fists. Dynamite on rock. There were explosions of blood. Lash Logan grunted and swore. He seemed oblivious of the girl's presence.

Dave knew this attack had more reason to it than just the carrying out of Jervis Manley's orders. Lash Logan hated him, and evidently had just been waiting an opportunity. This was it.

Dave felt terrific anger inside him as the other man swore. It was not good for Mabel to hear such language. Dave Markham, who had been in many a saloon brawl, was a bit of a puritan in some ways. Actually, he wished Mabel were not here to see the fight, but it could not be helped now.

He piled a hammer-like blow to Lash Logan's leathery face, saw the man stumble. He came in with another, stood over the man as he crashed to the dusty ranch-yard.

'Now git, or it will be worse for yuh!' said Dave thickly. The man half-scrambled to his feet again, hatred blazing in his face as he crouched with fists weaving savagely.

'Mabel, get along to the corral,' said Dave quickly. 'I sure don't like yuh to see a man make a doggone fool o' himself. An' this *hombre* is doing just that.'

'I'll wait, Dave.' She was pale, and not enjoying the spectacle. But she did not intend to leave men who were fighting because of her. Lash Logan came in again with his head down. He tried to butt

Dave in the middle. The foreman's hat had long since rolled in the dust. His dark, shaggy head came up under Dave's guard and rammed hard into the rancher's stomach.

Dave felt the agonising pain as it buckled him in two. He tried to fend off the other man, but he knew he was staggering to the ground.

He fell, and as he fell he put out a hand to steady himself. As his hand lay in the dust, Lash Logan stamped on it. Pain washed through the bruised hand, and Dave gritted his teeth. The dirty coyote could not fight fair.

With not a scrap of air in his lungs and a painful rasping in his throat, Dave made a Herculean effort to gain his feet. He slithered back to gain space, and jumped up with a contorted face.

He threw two blows at Lash Logan which had no steam. But they gained him time. He felt better. He gulped air, and decided to wade in and smash the other man.

Lash Logan had taken punishment earlier, so he had not escaped. Dave moved in to the panting man and got under the other's guard. He let go with all his weight – a right and then a left. Again a right and a left. The face before him twisted in agony. The man hissed like an old railroad engine. He sobbed and fell. A final blow from Dave carried him on his way to the dust of the yard.

Dave fell back when he saw that Lash Logan made no attempt to rise. The man lay shaking his head as if trying to clear the fog.

Blood dribbled from the corners of his mouth. He was not a pretty sight. Dave stood before Mabel, and said:

'Let's go. Sorry yuh had to see this, Mabel. I'm mighty sorry.' A few Double J waddies had appeared from the ranch buildings. They did not interfere. It had been a fight between men, and a fair fight on the part of one, at least. Such fights were not infrequent in a country where animosity flared into pitched battle, where words were merely the preliminary to battle, and not the sole weapons of the combatants.

Of Jervis or Frank Manley, there was no sign. It seemed Frank was out on the range. And Jervis was still with the retrieved cattle. Dave led his gelding to the corral, where Mabel saddled a cayuse. He wiped dust, sweat and blood from his face. He looked sombrely at the girl.

'That rannigan wanted that fight, Mabel. Yuh heard what he said about being a pal of Thatch Gillman? Wonder to me Jervis doesn't sack him. Maybe he will now that Gillman is dead.'

'I'll sure tell Jervis a thing or two,' said the girl indignantly. 'Imagine giving orders that I have to be protected! Who does Jervis think he is?'

Dave could have told her the answer to the last question, but he refrained. Jervis wanted Mabel.

He helped the girl saddle the cayuse, and they finally rode out of the ranch-yard. Dave saw Lash

Logan on the bunkhouse steps, but the foreman did not glance his way. Dave turned a contemptuous back on the man, and rode out across the sage.

They went down the trail by the creek that watered the valley. Cattle were grazing, and the scene was peaceful. The creek was a mere trickle at the moment, but when the rains came, as they would, it became quite a torrent. Tributaries from the hills fed the creek. It was the life blood of the valley. Without it the grass would wither and the soil lift with every passing wind until slowly the years turned the valley into sandy waste and scrub country. It had happened to other places in the West; this erosion of good soil into rivers and its lifting by strong winds.

After a while the fight dropped from their minds, and the two made plans. They were intimate, delightful plans. Perhaps they were a trifle bold. In his imagination, with this girl by his side, Dave Markham saw himself as a power in the valley. Maybe he would prosper and buy more land. And Mabel, the prettiest girl in the valley, would be the respected wife of a big rancher.

The buildings of the Lazy Cloverleaf came into view. He pointed out the little ranch-house with the smaller bunkhouse nearby, the corrals and the work he had done that day. But mostly he spoke of the future plans. He showed her the cottonwood trees, and regretted that there were not more to provide shade. One thing, you couldn't hustle the growth of cottonwoods.

The sun was sweeping down to the west now in a blaze of brassy glory. It was late afternoon. Time for coffee and scones, if there was anyone to make them.

He hollered for Ned Brant to come and be introduced. He got no answer.

'Mighty queer,' he said to Mabel. 'I left the old *hombre* splitting logs when I went over to see the Double J and Happy S cattle come down from the hills. I didn't say a word to Ned; jest rode off. Heck, I'm the boss, ain't I?'

'You're the boss,' she said, smiling. 'Sure. Wal, where is the old drifter?'

He went through the ranch-house, and that did not take much time because there were only three rooms. He took a peer into the bunkhouse, and one glance was enough there because the place comprised only one large room. Ned was not in his bunk or at a table. Dave strode over to the ramshackle barn which he intended to rebuild. He looked in, and every muscle in his body tensed with anger.

Ned Brant was lying on the hard earth floor as if dead!

SIX

PLAN FOR A POSSE

Dave was there in a flash, and he turned the old man over. There was a bullet wound in the old-timer's shoulder and another livid bloody scar across his forehead.

He felt for his heart. There was a faint beating. Dave licked his hand, tested for the old man's breathing. It came in bare, imperceptible sighs.

So Ned was alive.

Mabel had entered the barn before Dave could prevent it. She caught her breath as she looked at the old-timer.

'Who's done this? Who could it be?'

'Yuh needn't ask,' said Dave grimly. 'Can only be Slick Sadman and his rannies. I wish I'd killed that snake.'

'I'm with yuh, Dave. I'm beginning to hate that *hombre.*'

With Ned alive, the need for a doctor was imperative. 'Take my gelding and don't spare him,' he told the girl. 'Get Doc Tanner outa Pine City. They only got two docs an' he's the best. He's got to come out right away.'

'Will yuh take care, Dave?' she asked.

'Sure. I'm getting me another gun on my belt. Guess I need it. I'll take care of Ned while you've gone. I'd go to Pine City myself, but I reckon it wouldn't be safe to leave yuh here alone.'

And without wasting another second, Mabel was away, riding the gallant steeldust gelding as if it had wings. Indeed, with the light girl as a rider, the horse simply flew over the mesquite.

Dave carried the old-timer into the ranch-house and made him comfortable. He took care not to cause him any pain.

Once on a mattress and blanket, he looked closer at the wounds. He got a wet cloth and damped the head wound. To his great relief the bullet had not entered the skull. But the bullet had seared away skin and flesh and the wicked scar would stay for the rest of the old-timer's life.

Dave put his hand to his own scar under his hat; his was now healing. These head wounds, with their mess of blood, always seemed to the attacker a fatal wound.

But there was a bullet somewhere in Ned's

shoulder. It would be for the skilled hands of Doc Tanner to extract it.

With the oldster now more comfortable, Dave took a quick look round from the porch of the ranch-house. He had grimly buckled on another gun. The leather holster was just as worn and shiny as his other holster. Not always had Dave Markham worn one gun. He had taken to one gun simply because two-gun men were sometimes looked on with suspicion by law-abiding folk.

If Slick Sadman got in his way again, he would show him what he could do with two six-guns.

There was a brooding peace over the range. The sun was dropping now, a red orb still filled with brassy heat. Heat shimmers were rising from the ground. Cattle lowed in the distance. A jack rabbit scuttled across open ground. Of human beings there was not a sound in the vastness of land around him.

Dave went back to his vigil. He looked at the new, mahogany clock he had bought in Pine City recently. He wished Mabel would return with the Doc. There was a chance he could track down the men who had attacked Ned Brant. Maybe they had left a trail. But maybe they had completely vanished into the myriad ravines of the uplands.

And then he heard the pounding of hoofs. He started to his feet, knowing instantly that it was too early for Mabel to have returned with Doc Tanner. Though Mabel was a born horsewoman, the elderly Doctor proceeded with caution.

Dave looked through a window, not showing himself much. He saw six horsemen pounding towards the ranch in a manner which could only be described as hostile.

Slick Sadman's outfit of renegades, he decided, and reached for a rifle from the wall. He worked the bolt, saw it was fully loaded. He waited until a saddle-gun cracked, sending a bullet thudding into the log-built ranch. Then he aimed at one of the flying horsemen. The single shot winged past the rider, and Dave cursed the difficulties of aiming.

These riders were up to something. He narrowed his eyes, saw one or two of the outlaws who had been in the Last Chance Saloon during the gun-fight. The horsemen, spurring wild-eyed broncs, were keeping up a non-stop movement. They rode round the ranchhouse and the buildings like Indians.

Then Dave saw two galloping madly towards the ranch-house. They were dragging some inflammable material on draw chains fastened to their saddles. Even now the stuff was burning, fanned by the wind created as they moved. As Dave showed himself slightly at the window, a volley of shots was directed at him from the other riders. He had to duck back after pressing his rifle trigger once at the oncoming riders. Again with bad luck, he missed.

The intention was to fire the ranch buildings. Slick Sadman intended to burn his place to the ground as revenge. Dave had not seen the outlaw so far. Maybe he was not with his men. If he was not there, the riders were plumb tough *hombres* who evidently liked death and destruction because of some in-bitten complex.

Dave slipped round to another window, pushed the rifle muzzle through a slot and fired two shots rapidly at the oncoming riders dragging the burning stuff.

One man toppled immediately to the ground and rolled over and over like a sack of potatoes.

'One less,' muttered Dave.

But the other came right on, and rifle fire compelled Dave to flatten out of sight. When he looked again, inviting more lead, he saw with great anger that the other rider had stopped on the far side of the barn. At least that was Dave's surmise, for he could not see him.

A second later the horseman fed steel to his mount and appeared again at a great pace, making for the open country out of range of rifle fire. He was no longer dragging the burning brush.

Dave guessed at the trick. The man had left the burning stuff to fire the barn. The barn was near to the ranch-house, and flames would leap the short distance.

The rider did not get far. Dave took especial aim, in spite of the covering fire which was taking chips out of the wood around him. He pressed the trigger and the man took a headlong dive from his galloping mount.

'Got yuh, my bucko!'

But the fire at the barn was taking hold. He could see smoke billowing out on the hidden side. It was a ramshackle barn, but Dave did not intend to see it burn.

He came out of the ranch-house holding the rifle. He dashed to the cover of the barn amid a volley of shots. The members of the owlhoot brigade were still providing lead.

The riders had dismounted in the shade of the outer fringe of cottonwoods, and were using the great trees as cover. Before Dave could attend to the fire, which was taking hold quickly, he would have to disperse that gun shooting.

No small order. He was one man against four. He could not turn his back while he attempted to put out a fire.

But Dave was mad with rage. And in this mood he stood up and fired into the lurking figures in the cottonwoods.

He had no cover and he was risking his life. One shot could get him. But such was his rage, he forgot his usual cautionary tactics. He just stood up and shot it out.

He reloaded faster than lightning. He snapped off a shot at a lurking rannigan and heard the howl of rage and pain that went up. He saw another try to make for his horse, and Dave stopped that one dead in his tracks.

The other three darted for their horses with a rapidity that might have been comical under any other circumstances. They got on their mounts and frantically fed steel while Dave was shooting at the last fellow.

He gave them a fair fusillade to speed them on their way, and only then did he turn to the fire and smoke behind his back. There just was not time to pursue the riders. He had to attend to the fire. And Ned was still in the ranch-house.

The burning brush had been dipped in some inflammable substance, and was a mass of flame. Dave got the tip of a branch and whipped it clear of the barn. He saw the barn timber was on fire.

There was no water. He ran to the ranch-house, grabbed an axe and began to hack out the burning planks.

He roused a goodly shower of sparks, and flames spat into his face. But in the end he got the fire out. He pulled some timber free and stamped out the fire.

He swore at the rustler outlaw. If there was one thing that was darned certain, it was the fact that Slick Sadman and he would one day shoot it out. One of them would be dead.

But it would not be Dave Markham, he bet.

He went over and looked at the dead rannies. They were typical owlhoots. Both were half-

Mexican, if their sallow, hawklike features were any guide. Both had plenty of range dust on their clothes. Two six-guns lay in shiny cutaway holsters. No one would lose any sleep now that these two *hombres* were dead. No one would care about their names, their histories. They were dead men, in a country which had seen many men die in violence.

He looked through their belongings, but there was nothing that might be useful in the fight against Slick Sadman. Nothing here that would connect Thatch Gillman with the outlaw – or Lash Logan or even Jervis Manley, for that matter.

Dave was rather worried about Jervis. He had been on the fringe of the law. It only needed some little thing to tip the scales, and yet it probably needed very little to bring Jervis to his senses. With the death of Gillman, who had been blackmailing Jervis, it would seem that the part-owner of the Double J should be okay from now on.

Lash Logan seemed to be boastful of his friend-ship with the dead Gillman. No sense of shame there. That *hombre* would take some watching. But it was mostly Jervis's business.

As Dave was going through the dead outlaws' pockets, the sound of hoof beats came to him. He looked up. Mabel and Doc Tanner were riding up.

They reined in when they saw the dead men sprawled in the pasture beside the ranch-house, and Doc Tanner pushed his hat back. 'More dead 'uns! I hear yuh bin filling the town jail with bodies, Mister Markham!'

Doc Tanner liked his little jokes, almost all of which were gruesome. He liked to make the people shudder with tales of operations. He liked to dwell upon all the ghastly pains and aches the body was heir to. He was the most unconventional Doc in the unconventional West. If folks did not like his little wisecracks – wal, they could get themselves another doctor. There was only another one in Pine City, and he was always drunk.

'Yuh needn't waste any time on these galoots, Doc,' said Dave. 'I've got an old hand in the ranchhouse who needs your attention, an' he don't need any funny stories. Anyway, he's unconscious.'

'Unconscious, huh? Then he won't feel that bullet moving closer into the flesh. Most people yelp when they feel the bullet grinding on the bone. Kinda uncomfortable!'

Dave shook his head sadly. There was one thing; he knew Doc Tanner would have that bit of lead out in a jiffy. For all his strange talk he was a good doctor.

Mabel North looked at the damage to the barn. There was concern in her eyes. Already she associated herself with Dave and the Lazy Cloverleaf, and the damage made her mad. She looked at the rifle in his hands.

He told the story of the attack to the girl and the Doc.

'Some of Slick Sadman's rannigans with orders from that border rat to do me some damage. I guess a meetin' should be held in town to come to some agreement about getting rid of that varmint.'

Doc Tanner was busy on Ned's shoulder. He had Mabel busy too, bringing him hot water and clean cloths.

Until Ned could speak, there was no telling how it came he had been so badly shot-up. But the telling of the tale would make little difference. The facts were pretty plain. Ned had been shot – and probably not in fair fight.

After half-an-hour had passed Doc Tanner pronounced Ned would recover and be right as rain pretty soon.

'A tough old cuss, no doubt,' said the Doc. 'He never felt that bullet coming out because he was unconscious. Just as well, because the pain would ha' bin awful bad.'

'When yuh get back to town, tell the sheriff what happened here, Doc,' asked Dave. 'Sheriff Parsons oughta get a posse and go after that hellion. I'll ride with the posse, an' maybe we can get some other ranchers and their outfits to ride, too.'

'Then we'll ha' more dead bodies!' barked Doc Tanner. 'Wal, I guess I'll tell that no-good sheriff. They oughta make a feller like yuh sheriff.'

'Someday. I got plenty to do right now.'

Mabel glanced at Dave.

'You've got lots of things to do – we're going to get married soon, Doc!'

'Wal, that sure is a surprise! Gosh, but there are plenty o' pains coming outa marriage! You should see. . . .'

They both laughed in his face.

'Tell your old tales to the old maids!' laughed Mabel.

'Sure. You're killing us, Doc. Killing us!'

They both laughed him out of the house. He rode off into the crimson-shot evening, the sun glowing like a huge red orb on the horizon.

'Yuh oughta be getting back to the Double J,' said Dave. 'I oughta take yuh, but how the heck can I leave this old-timer?'

'Yuh haven't got to leave him. He was probably defending your place when those ornery cusses shot him. I'll be okay. It isn't far to the Double J.'

He kissed her suddenly, and laughed as he cupped her piquant face in his hands.

'Take care of yourself, honey, because yuh belong to me.'

'Adios!'

He saw her ride off until she was just a tiny figure in the magenta-shot distance.

He made preparations that night. The more he thought about it, the more certain he was that Slick Sadman would not stop at anything to see him dead. And the outlaw was not one to stick to the rules. There would be no fair stand-up fight.

Proof of that was shown in the fight that happened in the Last Chance Saloon. Slick Sadman had intended to trick him.

Obviously the rustler outlaw had had things his own way in the valley, retreating to the hills after taking cattle from various spreads. He just did not like the idea of Dave spoiling his play.

That night as silence descended over the valley from end to end, the ranch-house at the Lazy Cloverleaf was brightly lit. Through the uncurtained windows bright yellow light streamed from two oil-lamps.

Any passer-by, had there been anyone prowling the range at night, which was unusual, could see right into the ranch-house. But it seemed that Dave Markham got tired of staring out of windows, for pretty soon some yellow cloth was pinned up, serving as a blind.

Then any casual prowler might have seen the figure of a man sitting at a table evidently reading. The figure was motionless, as if the reader had much to scan.

After the first hour the figure shifted slightly and sat at the table from the other end. Dave Markham was evidently catching up on his reading, a very serious occupation on the ranges where books were few and far between.

But while the figure sat motionless, a man slipped out of an unlighted door. The man walked softly to the bunkhouse, keeping in the shadows.

He went inside, closed the door.

Dave Markham sat in the bunkhouse for two solid hours, staring through a wide slot at the lighted window in the ranch-house. The figure he had made up with such care with old mattresses and clothes kept its motionless attitude. The night got colder, and still he sat, gun in hand, waiting. Maybe he was acting on a hunch that had no foundation. Maybe he might sit up all night waiting for some drygulcher to take a pot-shot at the motionless figure; but, anyway, Dave felt it was a good bet that Slick Sadman would not leave him alone that night.

Slick Sadman knew that public opinion might suddenly make it hot for him. There might be a posse come out for him. The outlaw would likely want to strike at the man he hated while the folks of the valley were still unaroused.

Dave had the patience of all who were hunters and hunted. He was prepared to sit in the dark for a good many hours in the hope of catching a coyote. And not a four-legged one.

But even his stamina was wearing thin when hour after hour dragged by. It was cold, after the heat of the day, in the unlit bunkhouse.

And then he heard the faint sound.

It was the soft slither of boots against grass. It was a dry, rustling sound. Someone was coming, and the someone was purposely moving very silently!

Dave peered through the slot, but he could see nothing. There was nothing in the black, velvety night to excite suspicion. He strained, leaning forward to listen, holding his breath to catch the slightest sound.

Somewhere in the nearby foothills a coyote howled and an owl uttered a mournful cry. Dave silently slipped one gun from its holster.

He did not want to shoot at imaginary shadows. He thought it a good idea to wait until the other man pressed a trigger.

If he saw flame spouting, he would shoot at the source. Heaven help the drygulcher, for six .45 slugs would make an awful mess.

But the rustling shadow was taking it very slowly. If he wanted to shoot at the motionless figure outlined by the hastily pinned-up curtain, he had had every chance. He just was not shooting.

And then Dave saw the man, standing beside the corral. He was not standing in the cover of the cottonwoods as any drygulcher might expect to. The figure was absolutely motionless beside the corral poles.

Dave could have cracked the night air open with one of his six-guns. But he, too, could play a waiting game. In Montana he had stalked a man for seven days and nights . . . and down in the Big Bend country of Texas he had sat motionless for six hours behind two renegades in their camp. . . .

And then the night air was busted by four rifle shots which barked like sticks snapping but magnified a hundredfold.

Dave nearly pressed his trigger, aiming on the motionless figure by the corral, but he stopped himself instinctively without deliberate thought. For no shots had come from that man.

Dave swung. He looked into the cottonwoods. The bursts of gun-flame had come there. The flashes had died away.

The window in the ranch-house had shattered, and the dummy figure had fallen to one side.

'Good glass, too!' muttered Dave. 'And two rannigans laying for me. Huh!'

He swung out of the bunkhouse, moving softly. He came down the ranch-yard, moving in the deep shadow of the buildings all the time. Even as he moved, the figure by the corral moved too. The man walked rapidly down the length of the corral. But Dave was moving quickly, and as the shadowy man moved, he ran.

The man sensed him and broke into a run. Dave put all he knew into the last sprint. He fairly flew over the ground, and was on his man just as the fellow reached a clump of cottonwoods.

The other was a big man, and he turned as Dave leaped on him. He put up his hands as if to ward off blows. Dave collared him, and the other man struggled. It was pitch-dark, and Dave had no method of telling just who the intruder might be.

They struggled for a few minutes, and then the man said one word.

'Dave!'

It was an ejaculation more than anything.

Dave Markham stopped in dumbfounded amazement. 'Jervis!' he exclaimed.

The other man panted a little and said: 'Sure. It's me, Dave.'

'So yuh were laying for me, Jervis?'

'Yuh got it all wrong, Dave.'

'What in tarnation were yuh skulking for down by the corral?'

'Maybe yuh won't believe it, Dave, but I was worried about yuh!'

'Worried about me, huh? Come on, Jervis, give.'

'Sure. I saw yuh little setup with the window. Yuh didn't fool me none. Yuh see I know yuh smoke those quirlies all the time yuh sittin', Dave. Yuh wouldn't sit so quietly all that time without smoking a quirly.'

'Guess I fooled that other *hombre*, though. Yuh ain't told me why you were skulking in my ranch-yard this time o'night. Fine way to call on a feller.'

Dave was kidding Jervis. One thing, he knew the other had not shot at the dummy.

'The other *hombre* was my foreman, Lash Logan, Dave,' said Jervis sombrely.

'Yuh don't say!'

'Sure. I reckon I could ha' put some lead into him for shooting. I would ha' done, if that dummy had really bin yuh.'

'How come Logan wants to drygulch me?'

'Didn't yuh thrash him in front of Mabel?'

'Reckon I did. He asked for it. Is he mad?'

'He's a snake, Dave,' said Jervis gloomily. 'I've bin a plumb-fool. I can't sack that durned feller – he's got me cold over the Gillman affair. He knows a heck of a lot.'

'One thing, Jervis,' said Dave sternly. 'Yuh must take some responsibility for that *hombre*. Yuh gave him orders to throw out anyone who talked to Mabel. Don't yuh think Mabel can make up her own mind about things like that?'

'She seems to ha' made up her mind,' said Jervis bitterly. 'Yuh were kissing her, I hear. What's on your mind?'

Dave tensed with anger.

'Listen, Jervis. That's certainly my business, and I aim to tell yuh an' the whole durned world. But damn me if I'll tell yuh anything standing here.'

'Yuh don't have to tell me.'

'Maybe. But we will, an' to-morrow in some sort o' civilised surroundings.'

'Yuh aim to take her away from the Double J?'

'Since yuh ask – sure.'

'Is this spread anything like the Double J?' sneered Jervis.

Dave controlled his anger. 'It's mine and it'll be durned sight better before long.'

'Gonna build it up with bounty money-blood

money. Yuh told Mabel all that?' Jervis was really bitter, flinging taunts which Dave Markham would not have tolerated from any other man.

'I've told her everything. Yuh really mad at losing her, ain't yuh, Jervis?'

'She was something pretty great to me!' flung out the other. His voice was desperate. 'I'd ha' done anythin' – anythin', I tell yuh. Anythin' to – to – get her!'

'It's a matter which time will have to deal with,' said Dave quietly. 'Someone loses, someone wins. Yuh know that, Jervis.'

'Right! So I know it! Forget it!' Jervis snapped.

'Yuh haven't told me how come yuh know Lash Logan was all set to drygulch me!'

'It's simple. I saw him leaving the bunkhouse. I knew about the fight, an' it had me plumb worried. I know Lash Logan. He's a snakeroo. I wanted to see what he was up to, an' I jest followed him. He didn't see me none. I was all set to turn back when I saw him saddle his hoss an' set off for your spread.'

Dave smiled grimly.

'An' I was figuring Slick Sadman would show up! Sure is a surprising world. I guess I've made more enemies in this valley in a few days than some *hombres* make all their lives.'

'I wouldn't worry none about that. Yuh can take care o' yourself. I see yuh're packing two guns now.'

'Yeah. Did Mabel tell yuh about the fracas with Slick Sadman's outfit? They tried to burn down my ranch. Seems they kinda like to play with fire, those *hombres.*'

'They'll get yuh, if yuh try to buck those fellers single-handed,' warned Jervis.

'That's a matter o' opinion,' retorted Dave. 'But I sure reckon that old Sheriff Parsons oughta try to get those owlhoots outa those hills. Wonder to me the people round here put up with them so long.'

'Maybe if they put a bounty on Slick Sadman's head, yuh'd have a target worth risking somethin' for,' growled Jervis.

He received a warning look from the other man. 'I can kill that polecat without a bounty!'

'Then they oughta make yuh sheriff!'

'Yuh're the second feller who's told me that in the last few hours.'

'Would yuh take the office?'

They moved out of the shadows towards the light streaming from the broken windows of the ranch-house.

'Too much to do,' said Dave. 'And, anyway, the old sheriff has many friends who think things are all right the way they are.'

Dave snatched a few hours sleep that night sitting in a large old chair near to Ned Brant. His guns lay handy in case of interruptions. There were no lights.

By early morning the old drifter regained consciousness. He sat up in the bunk and groaned. His bleary eyes, set in a whiskered face, surveyed his surroundings and then his bandaged shoulder. He cursed.

'Those stinking polecats! Those durned owlhoots! Ef I get my gunsights on 'em, I'll shoot 'em to the ground, sure as my name's Ned Brant. Shot me down, they did! Left me dead, I reckon. Huh, they oughta look a bit closer at a dead man! Sometimes they are plumb alive!'

Dave grinned.

'Wal, yuh're alive, pardner. Doc Tanner dug a bullet out yuh shoulder, so go easy moving that arm. And yuh got a nice little scar by yuh head – same as me, but a bit worse, I reckon.'

'Looks like that Slick Sadman is lying up for a day or two,' rapped Ned. 'Those hellions who jumped me were without their mangy leader.'

'Slick Sadman got a bullet in his shoulder,' Dave reminded. 'But it won't lay him up for long.'

'No more than it will me,' grunted Ned.

He tried to roll out of the bunk, but Dave firmly pushed him back.

'Take it easy, old-timer. No fences to mend to-day.'

'By Gawd, yuh treat me like I was sick!'

Dave Markham rode into Pine City about midday. He had a plan, and after that plan he intended to go over and see Mabel. Then he would have the pleasure of telling Frank and Jervis that he intended to marry Mabel North and that Mabel was more than willing. Frank would be pleased, but he was not sure about Jervis. Dave rode into the town, along the dusty street, and then considered. He reckoned he ought to see the sheriff first.

He found the old man in his office, and straight away Dave launched out. He told the sheriff all that had happened in connection with Slick Sadman.

'I'm a rancher in this valley, Sheriff Parsons, an' I reckon that badman has had long enough run. What about getting a posse to collect this gent?'

Sheriff Parsons was not too pleased.

'We tried it before, Markham. That gun-hawk is plenty slippy. How the heck can we find him in those hills? He jest sees us coming miles away, an' then hits the trail. Them hills run back as far as any man can travel in days. I kin tell yuh what will happen if yuh get a posse. Right now I know what will happen. That galoot won't be seen nowhere, an' yuh posse will jest come back as empty-handed as it went out. No, sir! We'll git that feller some day, and that'll be when he makes a mistake. Some *hombre* will get him. Takes time, Mister Markham. Takes time!'

Dave smiled thinly.

'In the meantime he does any durned thing.'

He left the office, shrugging his shoulders. The sheriff might be right, and he might be getting

111

old. Of course it was all a matter of opinion. It would be a ticklish job hunting Slick Sadman in the mountains.

Dave stood on the boardwalk outside the office and hesitated. Should he tell the populace or should he just wander off after Slick Sadman himself?

In a way he was sick of the necessity to be always hounding down men. He would sooner he was at work out in the clean spaces round his spread, with Mabel by his side. But until a man could get set to work, the community would have to get rid of Slick Sadman.

He looked down the dusty street. Hot sunshine was drenching the town. There were many people in the streets, for all that. Men were coming in from distant ranches to get ready for an evening in Pine City. Many women were shopping from the stores.

He hammered on the tie-rail with the butt of his gun in an effort to gain attention. The people in the street gradually stopped beside him, brown, upturned faces looking inquiringly. In a very short time the street was crammed with folks and several buckboards were here and there with the owners and others standing up above the sea of faces.

'Folks, I don't want to take up a deal of your time,' he cried. 'But I think it right yuh should know I been in to see Sheriff Parsons about this Slick Sadman.'

At the mention of the outlaw, a greater silence fell over the crowd. Men looked significantly at each other. Women ceased their chattering and stared interestedly at the young rancher. Most people knew Dave Markham, even though he had been away for three years.

'I reckon it's high time this *hombre* was taken to a necktie party,' went on Dave. 'I suggested to the sheriff that we get a posse to hunt this galoot. But the sheriff thinks differently. He thinks it would be mighty difficult to get hands on Slick Sadman in the hills, an' he figures to catch the *hombre* when he comes down outa them hills. Now that may be right. But I don't think so.'

'What do yuh think?' called a voice.

'I reckon a posse oughta get together and chase that *hombre* out of the hills. Track him down until he either stands and shoots it out or he gets out of the country altogether.'

'Mister, yuh sure make it sound easy,' said one man in the crowd. 'But let me tell yuh, I bin on two posses to get that *hombre* an' we got neither sight nor smell o' him. He's one slippery feller.'

'Sure is,' said another. 'He'll taste lead sooner or later. Why, I heard yuh crossed his trail yourself, Mister Markham. Maybe yuh'll swap lead!'

There was a chuckle at this sally.

'Good idea,' drawled another voice. 'Maybe yuh fancy chasing Slick Sadman into them mountains yuhself.'

113

Dave looked quickly at the speaker. It was Lash Logan, standing in a buckboard, a sneering expression visible on his brown face even at a distance.

'I've been in the hills and killed two o' Slick Sadman's hands,' retorted Dave. 'And I'm hankering to go again. Maybe I'll kill some more rattlers. Maybe Slick Sadman has pardners in town who'll be mighty quick to let him know what is on my mind.'

'Maybe he has!' snarled Lash Logan. He added quickly: 'But I sure don't know them.'

'Yuh don't say!' drawled Dave.

'I'll go with yuh, Dave,' said a young voice.

It was Frank Manley. He sat his horse on the fringe of the crowd. Dave had seen him as he rode down the street.

'Thanks, Frank. Might take yuh up on that. The folks of Pine City don't seem to care much about chasing Slick Sadman from those hills.'

'We don't think much of rounding up a posse,' said a steady voice. Dave recognised the speaker as Bud Cornliss, a tophand with Charlie Kennedy's Happy S spread. 'Yuh see, Dave, it's bin tried before. But we're behind yuh in trying to get rid o' that owlhoot. If he ever crosses my trail I aim to shoot fast and straight. But I figure to wait until he does.'

That seemed to be the consensus of opinion. Dave was disappointed, but he realised folks had a right to their opinions and own ideas.

When the crowd dispersed, Frank Manley rode out of town with Dave.

'I was sure surprised to see yuh makin' speeches, Dave.'

'It was jest an idea. I was tryin' to wake the people up. Say, this town is getting sleepy!'

'I sure meant it, Dave, when I said I was behind yuh if yuh wanted a pardner to root out that badman.'

Dave thought deeply for a moment or two.

'Yuh oughta hear what Jervis says about that, Frank. He's yuh elder brother an'—'

'Yuh mean yuh think I should stay at home!' burst out Frank indignantly. 'Yuh think I'm a bit of a tenderfoot just because yuh and Jervis are a bit older than me! Tarnation, Dave Markham! If yuh—'

'Say – yuh'd waken a dead burro! All right, then, saddle a cayuse, get a grubstake, a saddle gun and two six-guns an' we'll hit the hills. I'll ride over with yuh to the Double J and inform yuh elder brother just what we intend to do.'

Frank grinned.

'Sure. But yuh don't want to see Mabel, do yuh?' jeered Frank.

Dave tried to bump him off his saddle.

'As I said – you're sure too young for many things, but wait till we hit the Double J. Plenty to tell yuh then. Only I want Mabel to be there.'

115

SEVEN

BENT FOR BOOTHILL

But there was a mixed reception for Dave and Frank at the Double J ranch-house. Jervis was undoubtedly hostile to the idea of young Frank Manley going into the upland country to track down Slick Sadman and his outfit. That he was with Dave Markham, would make it worse. Slick Sadman might ride out of trouble connected with Sheriff Parsons or a posse of indignant townsfolk, but the outlaw seemed hell-bent to kill Dave Markham.

And Mabel North was terribly uneasy about Dave's proposal to go into the hills. Like all women she wanted her man at home! Dave held her loosely with his arm round her shoulders. They were standing in the Double J ranch-house; a great red sun was shining through the ranch-window. Frank and Jervis were standing nearby. On Jervis's face was his obvious opposition to Dave's scheme to hunt Slick Sadman. To make matters worse, Dave announced that he and Mabel were to be wed.

'Sure like to congratulate yuh, Dave,' said Frank smiling. 'And you, too, Mabel. Sure seems like yuh still in the family, you marrying Dave.'

Jervis had to add his congratulations, but he found it hard. He licked dry lips, and he could not stand the sight of the girl's radiant face. He took to staring out of a window.

His thoughts were confused. He, too, had wanted this girl. He had proposed and been turned down. He fought with conflicting emotions, trying to conquer hate and bitter thoughts. In the end he turned suddenly to the others and said:

'If yuh bent on going up into the hills after this hellion, Frank, I'm going with yuh.'

'That's the feller!' exclaimed Frank, thumping his brother's back.

Secretly, Jervis's thoughts ran like this: 'If some of us don't come back – if it's Dave or me that tastes lead – Mabel will turn to one of us. That way, I've got to go along with Dave and Frank. I'll take the risk along with them. I promised the Old Man to look after Frank, anyway. He's just a kid for all his height – not even twenty-one yet.'

'We'll spend three days up in those hills,' Dave was saying. 'If we don't get sight of Slick Sadman in that time, it means the *hombre* is on the run.'

'He'll try every trick to get yuh,' said Jervis harshly.

'We know a few tricks, too,' said Dave quietly.

'Do – you – you – have to go, Dave?' asked Mabel. He turned to her in great earnestness.

'If this man is left to do what he likes, it is good-bye to law and order in this valley. Other owlhoots, from the borders, will drift in. They'll think the people round here are easy money. The news will get around. I've seen it happen before. This galoot has to be stopped as a warning to any others. Maybe, too, the townsfolk are right, and Slick Sadman would run from a posse. But I'm banking that he won't run from me. He hates me.'

'That means he'll try to get yuh,' she faltered. 'Oh, Dave!'

But she was a Western woman. She could not stop a man from a man's duty.

'If he tries to kill me, that will mean his own end!' vowed Dave. 'Seems like this is the only way to get rid of the hellion.' Frank and Jervis were silent, knowing that Dave was practically using himself as a decoy – but, at any rate, a decoy that would shoot back!

They set off within an hour, even though the midday sun was pouring down its heat. They had

grub, rifles, six-guns and horses. They were determined men who could live in the open country
and there was nothing more they needed.

Dave and Jervis knew the trail to the upland
meadow, and they figured that they would find
fresh sign round that territory. If there was a lead,
it might be found there. They did not expect to
find Slick Sadman's outfit camped there, however.

They moved quickly at first over mesa and then
to scrub country. As they came into the first of the
rising foothills, they slowed the horses to a walk.
The way led up ravines and broken rock outcrops.
It was hot plodding work, with dust rising
constantly from the horses' hoofs. Soon the riders
were coated. They were parched, too, but counted
upon finding water in the upland meadow which
would slaken their own thirsts and the horses'.

If Slick Sadman had another camp in the hills,
they saw no sign of it, and if he had men posted as
lookouts, they gave no sign of sighting them. Dave
and Jervis kept an eye open continuously.

They dare not be ambushed. To be drygulched
now would make the whole expedition the laugh-
ing-stock of Pine City. If their plan came off, maybe
the folks of the town would see that they had a new
sheriff. Even the deputy seemed infected with the
same complacent caution. It was not the way to get
things done.

They rode round by the cattle trail into the
upland meadow just as the sun sank like a red ball

of fire. It was a fierce sun, leaving shimmering waves of heat rising from the earth. The earth would be warm all night, and early in the morning the sun would bring out its brassy glare again. It was a man's country, and being in the hills made it no cooler. At this time of the year, even the winds blew like the hot breath of an oven.

There were no cattle left in the meadow. The whole lot had been rounded up and taken to the valley below. Had Slick Sadman counted on selling the beef to the rail-road gang some thirty miles away in the Chuhunger Canyon, he would be sadly disappointed.

'Could camp here,' said Jervis. 'There's the lean-to. Some sort o' shelter from a stray mountain-cat.'

'Not a bad idea if one is on guard all the time,' agreed Dave.

'Yuh can leave the first guard to me,' boasted Frank. 'I'm still good for a scrap or a night's riding.'

'Yeah? Wal, we do no more ridin',' said Dave. 'An' yuh can have the first guard, an' good luck to yuh.'

They inspected the lean-to. It was a crude structure of logs, wattles and mud. The beaten earth floor was reasonably clean. Sometimes such places rather resembled cattle sheds.

They sat down and got a fire started in the adobe fireplace. If there was smoke, they did not care. They more or less wanted Slick Sadman to find them. They were forthright men with a job to do, and subtle methods were pushed aside.

They got bacon and flapjacks cooking, and soon there was an odour which would tempt those with ulcers.

For hungry men, there was but one thing to do, and that was get it down.

Knowing the smoke was rising through the hole in the shack, they kept a look-out even while they ate. They did not want to be bushwhacked while eating bacon and flapjacks.

The sun finally sank reluctantly in a red grave, and the heat waves subsided. There were long shadows in the hills, and a silence which was only broken as a coyote howled at the swiftly falling night.

There was nothing to do but watch. Soon two of them would sleep, but not the third. They were there to tempt the badmen, but not to offer themselves as easy bait.

Meanwhile, in the valley below, things happened at the Double J which would have sent Dave Markham crazy with fear.

Lash Logan called on Mabel when everything was quiet except for the buzz of conversation in the cowboys' bunkhouse.

Mabel was quietly busy in the ranch-house. She had a room to herself on the east wing. The ranch-house was pretty big by comparison with, say,

Dave's small place. There were many rooms with real glass windows and skin rugs. Some of the more primitive went to bed with sundown.

There were always things to do for the girl, but this night she had determined to do some sewing for herself. A girl who was going to be married had to get darned busy with the needle!

There was no warning knock – no sound until she looked up to find Lash Logan over her.

One look at his face was enough to raise her fears. 'What do yuh want?'

'I'd sure like yuh, but that's not why I'm here,' sneered the man.

'Go away – before I scream!' she breathed.

There was a shot-gun on the wall, and it was always loaded, she knew. If she could only get it. . .

But Lash Logan intercepted her glance, and he laughed grimly. 'Yuh not tryin' anything funny, Miss Mabel. I've got a job to do. . . .'

He leaped on her and circled her with his arms. One large, soiled hand clamped on her mouth even as she tried to scream.

Lash Logan was a big man, hardened by years of toil. He could handle her as if she was a child. He forced her to the door, across the room. She struggled like a fury.

'Won't do yuh much good to fight!' he hissed. 'Yuh're going with me fer a midnight ride. Yuh going into the hill country – though I'm not taking yuh. We're meeting some pals o' mine. Now git goin.'

He pushed her out into the ranch-yard where a horse was tied. There was nobody around. The cowpunchers were playing cards in the bunkhouse, and were very much occupied. There was not much moon even if someone had been around to see the strange sight.

Lash Logan simply threw the girl on to the saddle and, while he held her, he jumped to the leather himself. Within a second he had the horse galloping out of the ranch-yard, swerving at a hell's pace past the pepper trees, down across the mesa. It was a reckless ride. The mesquite was no place for fast night riding. If the horse stumbled, they might take a nasty fall.

Out in the open prairie, she could scream for all her might. It made no difference. With every minute the thundering hoofs of the horse were putting yards between her and possible rescue. No one was out in the night – except, perhaps, renegades who travelled in the dark.

Lash Logan was possibly made reckless by the very nature of his exploit. He was a rannigan who had hovered on the fringe of the law for some time. With this exploit he definitely put himself beyond the law – if ever the law learned he was responsible. And there was a strong possibility that the law would never know what had happened to Mabel North that night. Though they might guess.

For Mabel would never see the Double J again!

Out in the wide spaces, he removed his hand from her mouth. Instinctively she screamed, but it only served to amuse him in a savage way.

'There ain't nobody tuh hear yuh!' he snapped. 'Yuh can holler the sky open – it don't make no difference.'

'Where are yuh takin' me?' she gasped.

'To see a pal,' he said, chuckling. 'A pal o' yuh man friend, Dave Markham.'

'What do yuh mean?'

'I got orders – and some good money – tuh take yuh tuh Slick Sadman. Say, yuh needn't get worried. Slick is up in the hills, an' these gents got orders to take yuh there. Nacherally they'd sure like tuh steal a kiss, but I guess they won't because Slick is an ornery gent if his orders are disobeyed. Sure would like tuh have a bit of fun with yuh myself. But I reckon there ain't time. I'm late already with my meeting with those night riders of Slick's.'

She broke into renewed struggles at this hideous information. 'Dave Markham will kill yuh for this!' she panted.

'Maybe that *hombre* will get killed himself,' snapped Lash Logan. 'At any rate he's sure riding into trouble. There are ways and means of letting Slick know what's going on in this town, and Slick knows all about Dave Markham's ridin into them hills. He won't get far. Pretty soon there'll be some corpses in those ravines.'

The horse thundered its way over the plains. At this pace it was only a matter of minutes before she was handed over to the outlaw's men in the rising ground.

'Yuh can't get away with it!' she warned. 'People know now yuh were a pal of Thatch Gillman, and they'll guess.'

'Yuh talk like a crazy owl!' he said savagely. 'I've a good mind tuh teach yuh a lesson! Shut yuh mouth about Gillman.'

'He's dead!' said the girl spiritedly. 'And all *hombres* like him will be dead pretty soon. There'll be a clean-up.'

He struck her across the mouth. She did not moan but suffered the blow in silence. He urged the horse on with spurred steel and curses.

'I can give yuh money—' she began bitterly.

'I said, shut up! Yuh ain't got enough money!'

'What good will this do Slick Sadman?' she said desperately.

'Yuh a hostage, I guess.'

'I'll kill myself sooner than let Dave be tricked.'

'Yuh won't get the chance. What Slick intends to do with yuh is his business. Maybe he jest intends to make Dave Markham mad. I sure hope he kills that ornery galoot!'

'Yuh hate Dave, but yuh afraid to stand up to him!' She was determined to taunt him.

He struck her again and cursed. He was pretty strung up with his exploit. Maybe he had qualms.

They met up with the night riders at the edge of the mesa. There were coulees and broken ground providing shadow, if shadow were needed. The men were lurking there, and they made themselves known as Lash Logan spurred his horse up a slope. The three night riders appeared as black shapes on the ridge of the slope. Lash Logan gave a cry and was answered by a harsh: 'Right, pardner!'

The horses met up, and the girl was transferred to the saddle of a big mare. The man who rode behind her was a border breed, and he smelled like all his kin. His hairy hands gripped her as he chuckled evilly.

Lash Logan muttered a farewell, wheeled his horse and galloped off into the night. He was bound for Pine City, where drunken friends would alibi him. Also he felt the need for raw whiskey.

If the flight across the mesa had been frightening, the laborious climb into the hills was a nightmare. The men who rode were sure of their path. They rode in silence as befitted men accustomed to riding the owlhoot trail. The horses picked a way over loose shale and rocky paths where only mountain cats ever moved. Mabel was completely lost. She had never been so far into the hill country. And the black ridges seemed all alike in their monotonous outline,

After a while she gave up her futile struggles. She was completely in their power, and to wear herself out was silly. She just had to keep her wits about her. Somewhere there might be a chance to turn a trick on these men.

But it seemed a very weak chance!

*

Frank Manley had finished his watch and nothing had happened except the murmurs of slowly stirring wind among the cedars and juniper trees. Other noises had reached his intent ears, but they were merely the sounds of creatures of the night – and four-legged ones, at that!

Dave took over, though Frank was reluctant to waken him. He only did so because he feared the strong words the other man would use if he found the first guard had taken on more time than he should.

Dave Markham slowly rolled a cigarette, lit it with a shaded match. He stared reflectively over the black shapes of the trees pressing down from the hills into this little valley. He wondered about Ned Brant in the Lazy Cloverleaf ranch-house, and he hoped the oldster would be able to fend for himself. He guessed Ned would make out all right. His wounds were not so bad now that he had attention.

From Ned Brant, he fell to thinking of Mabel. She sure was the prettiest girl in the valley! That she would share his lot was the greatest thing that could happen in his life. He just had not the words to express what he really felt about her.

And then it came – a rustling sound on the left, among the scrub timber. Someone was moving through the dry undergrowth! Someone was risking plenty in the dark, formidable scrub timber unless the rustling was made by some wandering bear. But Dave thought it was no bear. Bears did not move at night – unlike the mountain cat.

He waited, hoping to see some outline, some shape that would determine just who was making the stealthy sound. But beyond a sense of someone being out there in the dark pines and cedars, he could make out nothing. He slid his gun out, ready.

There was nothing to aim at. Not a durned thing. The rustling sound stopped. The *hombre* out there was pretty tough to travel through such rough ground at night.

Then came a dull thud as a rock pitched into the dusty earth beside the shack. Grimly Dave peered at the vague night shapes. Had he seen the slightest movement, he would have shot at it.

He wondered why the man had pitched a rock near to the lean-to. That it was a man, there was no doubt now. Bears just did not wander at night and pitch rocks.

There did not seem much sense in the play either. Dave waited, grim, tense. He heard the rustling for a moment more, and then it seemed to vanish in the distance. The night hawk was leaving! Dave felt sure that all he had done was to pitch a rock at the shack. There was no burning, or else he might have supposed it was another attempt to throw some inflammable material at the shack. It was pretty puzzling, but there was some significance.

He considered making a search out there in the dark, but he paused. This could be a trick. Some *hombre* might be waiting for him to show a light. The rustling sounds of departure might not be just what they indicated.

The more he thought about it, the surer he was that the thrown rock was intended as a lure. He grinned in the darkness. He reckoned he was not falling for that trick.

He waited, thinking that the man or men out there might be disappointed at the lack of success of their trick and show themselves more openly. But no further sounds came. This was pretty puzzling.

He felt safe in assuming the owlhoots would not give up because of the failure of one trick. To prowl through the scrub timber at night was a risky game at the best, and just to pitch a rock near the shack was not much of a play. He could have bet a lot that the men would try another trick.

But the brooding silence of the country was unbroken. Even the coyotes had given up howling.

After a score of minutes had ticked by with deadly monotony, Dave became convinced the man had indeed gone.

This just made the whole thing even more

puzzling!

Dave waited out his whole watch and then woke Jervis Manley. In a low whisper he told him about the mysterious play.

'Sure means the rattlers know we're here,' grunted Jervis. 'For me, I figure they'll try tuh rush this shack just before dawn. We'll be drygulched.'

'This is where we make a good play,' drawled Dave. 'Glad yuh think we'll be drygulched right here. Kinda clinches things in my mind.'

'What the heck do yuh mean?'

'I'm bankin' these *hombres* out there think the same way as yuh do, Jervis. I admit it is a good conclusion to think we are tenderfeet in this hill country. By sitting here like a bunch o' nesters, we look pretty green. Maybe Slick Sadman will figure it a good idea tuh attack at dawn. I sure hope so.'

'What do yuh figure, Dave?' Jervis looked sharply at the other man. There were worried lines etched in his face. A faint bit of light from the sky showed the haggard look in his face. Jervis Manley was not sure of himself.

'Wal, I guess we jest won't be squatting in this shack, that's all! But we sure got to make the owlhoots think we are. Then we turn and give them hell.'

Relief showed in the other's face for an instant. Then: 'How yuh goin' to do it, Dave? What's the details?'

'We get out now – like Apache Injuns. That

means no noise – not a durn squeak! But we leave a good fire a-smouldering with plenty o' smoke coming out o' that hole in the roof. And maybe a little light glowing – as if we were chancing a bit light! All the time we are hidden up in that scrub timber – and I mean hidden!'

'Sure. I get yuh,' said Jervis slowly. 'Then we drygulch those *hombres*!'

'In a sense. At least we'll give 'em a chance to shoot it out. That's more than the pack rats will give us, I reckon.'

'Seems a good idea,' said the cautious Jervis.

'It's jest as I said – we've got tuh lure those *hombres* on. Make some coffee, and then we'll git, pronto.'

They made strong hot coffee in silence, using the water they had collected a few hours ago. They wakened Frank, told him of the plan. Dave told the youngster about the rock that had been pitched near the shack.

'Sure would like tuh know what that rannigan was up to,' muttered Dave. 'I don't understand it, an' I don't like a thing I can't figure out.'

They drank the steaming beverage, and then set about making a fire that gave off plenty of smoke. They lit a rough, improvised wick swimming in an inch of bacon fat in the bottom of an old can they found. It gave a weird yellow glow through the lean-to. Yellow light cast a pale beam through the paneless window. Slick's side-kicks would see that light if they were around! The three men got out stealthily by a rear door. They even spent a few minutes cautiously opening the door inch by inch so that it would not creak. They moved like Indians from the rear of the shack and moved softly into the scrub that led to the timber clothing the hill.

They carried rifles and six-guns, but they left the horses tethered nearby the shack. If the outlaws saw the horses still tethered it would lend credence to the idea that the men were still in the shack.

Still puzzling about the apparently meaningless rock thrower, Dave led the way up the slope. They were in the scrub timber now, and the soil was loose, enabling them to move without noise, though somewhat laboriously.

He found a spot not too far from the shack where two fallen pine trees criss-crossed each other.

'This is it,' he muttered. 'Get a rough wickiup made to cover yuh. A few branches, then cover it with leaves and anythin' yuh can find. Yuh can get a bead on the shack and all the ground around it from here.'

'What do yuh mean, talking like yuh weren't with us?' demanded Frank. Dave grinned.

'Just that. I ain't going to be with yuh. I'm going back into that shack and I want another six-gun.'

'Tarnation! What's the idea?' spluttered Frank. 'I thought we figured to drygulch them *hombres* from here?'

'Sure. That's your job. But those hellions will be suspicious if they get no answering fire from the shack. So I aim to provide some lead. I want another six-gun. A clever *hombre* can tell from the bark of a gun just how many guns are firin' even when they are the same bore and fired with the same powder. I aim to make those *hombres* think at least three guns are spitting lead. Yuh two up here will get the drop on those hellions with the rifles.'

'An' those snakeroos will get the drop on yuh with rifles,' remarked Frank crossly. 'That shack is thinner than a Mexican dollar.'

'That sure remains to be seen,' said Dave.

'Yuh tricked us intuh goin' up here,' rapped Frank. 'Why the heck couldn't yuh say what yuh had in mind down in that shack?'

'Because yuh would start an argument. This showdown is particularly mine. I aim tuh take the lead my way.'

And then he was away with long strides, having taken one of Jervis's six-guns.

He came down the hill and crept into the rear of the shack satisfied that he had made no sound and that it was still dark enough to hide his movements. He had halted every twenty yards for a brief moment, straining his ears to hear any sound made by any stranger. But it seemed that the upland meadow, encompassed by the hills, was deserted. The rock-throwing *hombre* of a few hours ago had maybe gone to join his pals.

That meant Slick Sadman's outfit was not far away. Few men could travel far in this broken country at night. Many men would never even attempt it.

Dave made himself comfortable by the paneless window. He drank the remainder of the coffee, and grinned at the thought of the indignant Frank up there on the hillside.

Once or twice he gave thought to the rock-thrower, but in the end he tried to forget it. Dawn would come with its usual swiftness, and he would have to be mighty alert.

He stirred the fire, sending up a good volume of smoke and sparks. He hoped the owlhoots would come before it got unbearably hot in the shack. That they would come, he had no doubt.

He laid one six-gun at a rough slot beside the end of the shack, and another gun at the far end. He stood by the rough square that served as a window in the middle of the lean-to and held his other gun ready. He intended to move around, firing from different angles, and he did not want to carry three guns.

Then all at once the sun seemed to appear in the east, sending fiery claws streaking out on the horizon. The night was lifting in its usual speedy manner.

He was alerted, searching the scrub timber that straggled down to within twenty yards of the clearing and the meadow.

And then he saw the scarf on the ground just five yards away from the lean-to. The scarf was wrapped round a rock. He stared while the colour drained from his face. He knew that scarf instantly. It belonged to Mabel North!

The full significance sank in his mind like a flash. The skulking rock-thrower during the night had some significance now. The outlaws had the girl! That was the only conclusion. The scarf had been left there knowing full well that it would taunt the men who saw it. Dave gripped his gun in fury. He could only guess what had happened, but somehow Mabel was in danger.

And then a voice from afar hailed him.

'Markham, yuh skunk! Can yuh see yore girl's little scarf? Can yuh see it, yuh ornery polecat? Ef yuh can, well durn yuh eyes. It's all yuh'll ever see of the gal again! We got her!'

It was Slick Sadman's harsh voice, drunk with triumph. Nothing could be seen of the man. He was hidden somewhere in the scrub timber just above the cattle trail and to the left of Frank and Jervis. The man was gloating. He was there himself to make sure he saw the end of his enemy.

Dave could only stand tense with rage. He simply ached to get to close quarters and shoot it out, but there was nothing to aim at. His hands were stiff, but his finger was ready to squeeze death at any man.

But if Slick Sadman thought he had the drop on

three men in the shack, he was wrong. Dave could only wait until the attack began. He was sure the outlaw leader would not pass up this chance to send to Boothill three men who opposed him.

Slick Sadman evidently had means of knowing all that went on in the valley and Pine City. It seemed the man had spies. But maybe the approach of Dave, Frank and Jervis had been noted the night before.

'Yuh got nothing to say, Markham? Don't yuh believe we got yore little gal?'

Dave found his voice and let his fury blaze. An instinct warned him that it was better to let the outlaw leader think he had the men cooped up in the lean-to.

'I can hear yuh, Sadman!' he bawled. 'Why don't yuh come out in the open, yuh yellow-backed rattler? Ha' yuh got to skulk under stones all the time?'

He wanted to arouse the other to anger. Mostly he wanted to get a bead on the snake. Even if it meant risking his life. He would risk anything to kill Slick Sadman. And yet he had to keep out of the way of lead. Mabel had to be rescued.

'Yuh got it coming, Markham!' shouted Slick Sadman, with sheer venom making his words indistinct. 'Yuh'll know all about it soon. We got yuh an' yuh pals cooped like a lot o' wolves. Durn yore blasted hide! Yuh'll yell for mercy before we ha' done with yuh. Yuh sure spoilt my play in this territory.'

And then there was silence. It was a silence which cloaked the approach of stealthy men armed with six-guns and rifles.

Frank and Jervis, hiding up on the hillside, would have heard the exchange of remarks. They knew their play. They would lie low until they got a definite line on their men.

Slick Sadman would soon know that only six-guns spoke from the shack. He might think that odd, that men should come into the hills to hunt him with rifles, but maybe he would not think too much about it in the heat of exchanging lead.

The silence continued, and it was a grim moment for Dave. He could not help thinking about Mabel. It shook him to think of her in the power of these renegades. This was something he had not reckoned with. He wondered just how Slick Sadman had managed to get the girl. There was more trickery, he supposed. This outlaw was sheer snakeroo. And then hell broke loose!

Rifle fire began to spurt at the shack. It was a flimsy structure, and Dave found the prospect of random bullets thrusting through the walls and roof pretty grim. But he had known what to expect when he returned to the shack. It was easy to hit a solid object like a shack, and it did not need a direct hit to break a man's nerve. The Indians had first tried this method when attacking encampments. They lifted their rifles high so that the lead would rain down on the roof.

Slick Sadman certainly knew all the tricks. A bullet whined through the open window and dug into the opposite wall with a thud that was distinctly audible. Another hit the fire, scattering ashes in all directions. Some were steel-jacketed shells; others lead from six-guns.

Dave chanced a grim look through the window, saw a man dodging behind a tall cedar pretty near to the shack. He squeezed off a bullet that chipped wood inches from the man's head. Dave cursed at the miss, forgetting such accuracy with a six-gun at such a distance was pretty good – especially in the flurry of battle.

But he cursed all the same, because he was in a killing mood. He wanted to kill as he had never wanted before in his life. There was an itch in his finger to see men die.

He stepped quickly to the far end of the shack and whipped off two shots from that angle. He wanted to show the outlaws that there was firing from all angles. Soon the men would see that only six-guns were firing, and try to get nearer for an accurate shot.

He had to flatten out as steel-jacketed shells whanged into the cabin. They missed him by inches. He breathed deeply, and relieved his feelings by some good old-fashioned curses.

He chanced another rapid glance through the window. There was a battered Mexican sombrero jutting behind a slab of rock. Dave unleashed two bullets and saw the hat sag out of sight. Dave ducked to the floor as an answering volley chipped the window frame to splinters. But he judged by the way the man's hat had fallen that the *hombre's* head had been inside!

Also he had seen some movement among the galoots to get in closer. That was just what he wanted. It would not do to scare them off with too much good shooting.

He set back for a moment, lying on the earth floor with his head grimly down. Then, tired of playing doggo, he scrambled slowly towards a crack at the end of the cabin. He had to give the impression that three men were in the shack.

He loosened off two more shots with the six-gun, and then scrambled along the earth floor on his knees to the other end. He flung hot lead rapidly at two bobbing heads visible through the crack among the scrub timber.

That would be the end of his shooting, he thought grimly. If no shots came from the shack, Slick Sadman's men would think some of the doomed men were dead or dying. They would get out openly into the clearing, and that would give Frank and Jervis a chance to fling steel-jacketed bullets.

So far he had not heard the boom of guns from the hillside. When they opened out they would bring consternation to the outlaws. Dave lay down, thinking this was a heck of a way to fight or die. But Slick Sadman had to be matched with his own tricks.

He could not help his thoughts returning to Mabel. Somehow there had to be a way to get the girl out of the outlaw's hands. After a minute he got tired of simply lying on the floor hoping to dodge a bullet. It seemed most of the firing was coming from the front of the shack. Maybe it would be a good idea to get out at the rear of the shack and fight in the open. Maybe he could meet up with Slick Sadman himself that way.

As Dave darted out the rear, he heard the boom of rifles on the hillside. Frank and Jervis were opening up. Some of the owlhoot outlaws must be in the open now.

Dave reached the cover of some jack pine without drawing fire. He had his two six-guns with him. He had inadvertently left Jervis's gun in the shack.

He began to move cautiously round the area of the shack. He wanted to reach higher ground so that he could see everything. Right where he was, the shack obstructed the view.

He moved slowly and yet methodically, and soon had reached a knoll of higher ground which formed part of the bottle-neck mouth to the upland meadow.

He could see heads moving among the scrub and timber further ahead in the bottle-neck hills. He wished he was nearer, or that he had a rifle. His six-gun would just not carry that far.

It seemed that the attackers did not realise he was out in the open. They had not seen him. They might easily think that the lack of firing from the shack was due to the fact that the men inside were finished.

This might be good to Slick Sadman, but he would find his mistake. On the other hand they might think that reinforcements had arrived and were firing from the other hillside.

Dave could see spurts of rifle flame from the place where Frank and Jervis were entrenched. Two men, caught in the open, had taken refuge behind rocks and were returning Frank and Jervis's fire. It was a rifle battle. Slick Sadman would soon discover that the men were not in the shack.

In a sense, the strategy had served to draw the outlaws out of the scrub timber. Already two men sprawled dead, caught by Frank and Jervis's rifle fire. Even as Dave scrambled quickly through the loose soil, the outcome of the battle below was decided. The two men caught behind the rocks, which barely gave them cover, had chanced it once too often. A bullet from Frank's rifle drilled a neat hole through the head of one. The other tried to run in panic, and Jervis got him easily.

Dave could see a general withdrawing of Slick Sadman's hands. He wished he was nearer. He plunged on, risking drawing attention to himself.

But the outlaws did not notice him. They were busy giving shot for shot at the fire from the concealed men on the hillside.

And then Dave got close enough to draw on one *hombre* who was plunging through scrub and thicket to gain an advantage point. The man just threw up his hands as he died with a slug in his head!

Dave wondered where Slick Sadman was hiding. He hoped he would run into the bad *hombre*.

Dave risked running into an ambush. He was now right among the outlaws. They had scattered and were hiding singly behind cedars, rocks, and fallen trees.

At the sound of his gun one man suddenly shoved his head round a tree bole and snapped a six-gun at Dave.

But his hand was not quick enough. Dave's gun barked a second after sighting the *hombre* and a second before the other's gun exploded. The two shots seemed simultaneous, but the man behind the tree sagged sideways. His gun slipped from a nerveless hand. His shot had gone wide with the thud of Dave's bullet into his heart!

The exchange of lead brought shots from other hidden outlaws, and Dave had to dive into a clump of cactus scrub. He held his breath and his fire, hoping the men would be unsure.

It seemed that they were. Dave raised his head for a quick glance. What he saw he did not like.

The outlaws were on the run!

Two men were already on horses, slithering the snorting animals down the slope to the mouth of the little valley. Another was reaching for his horse. Dave ran like a madman down the slope and got within range of the escaping hellion. He let the man have it right in the neck, and the man fell with a howl of anguish, rolling in the soil and fallen pine needles.

There was the mixed sound of hoof-beats and sundry rifle and six-gun shots. At the bottom of the slope, among the clay and shale track, the rustlers were feeding steel to the mounts.

It seemed they were all getting out!

Dave saw Slick Sadman urging two men to stay. By the attitude of the owlhoot leader, he was mad with rage. Dave came down at a breakneck speed, dodging from boulder to boulder, slithering among fine soil and pine needles. A volley from the outlaws as a last gesture as they turned to ride out did not stop him. He stood up and fired back.

But Slick Sadman's men were getting out.

The neat ambush they had hoped to spring had not come off. The rifle fire from the hillside had disconcerted them. And Dave's appearance, after they had assumed him dead in the shack, had sent them into flight.

Most of Slick Sadman's hands were men of the border breed. Rough, callous fighters when things were fixed on their side, they still had not that heroic quality that sent men in to fight when odds were greatly stacked against them.

Dave watched them ride out with rage in his heart. He had set his mind on killing Slick Sadman in this battle, but here was the *hombre* riding out!

There was nothing Dave could do but run back for his horse. He came tearing down to the cabin as Frank and Jervis came through the scrub timber, rifles ready.

'The hellions have gone!' snapped Dave. 'Yuh heard that rattler saying' about Mabel. They got her somewheres.'

'A few of the galoots will not walk outa here again,' jerked Frank. 'We got two. How about yuh?'

'Two, I guess. I don't know!' said Dave worriedly. 'Let's git the hosses. We've got to keep sight o' them hellions.'

They rode out of the upland meadow – three men with a single purpose. They would rescue Mabel North from the hands of the outlaw band if they expended their lives in doing so!

EIGHT

FIGHTIN' MAN'S
FAREWELL

Mabel North was a girl who had been raised on a hard-living cattle ranch. She had been raised by old Tom Manley, Frank and Jervis's father, when her own father had died, and he had brought her up kindly but hardily.

The long journey through to this camp in the hills had been arduous, but she was not broken in spirit. She could endure plenty if there was the slightest chance of escape.

But just before Slick Sadman had set off with his men he had told her how he had Dave Markham and the others cooped up in a shack in the mountain meadow.

'Those polecats will rue the day they ever came

ridin' into these hills. We'll just shoot them to ribbons and leave the remains for the vultures. This will sure be a lesson to those townsfolk. Reckon they can't have much mountain sense tuh stick in that shack all night. We got 'em cold. We gave yuh friend a little reminder that yuh're in our hands. He'll sure die happy.'

She had seen the outlaw band ride off – about seven or eight strong. They had rifles. She feared for the three men in the upland meadow. Slick Sadman was a ruffian who had spent years in the hills – because no town would afford him shelter, and he was wanted by the law. But this seemed, to her mind, to give the bandit an advantage. He had plenty of hill-sense. Could Dave Markham cope with the other's cunning?

She was left in charge of two half-Mexicans, who leered at her as she lay bound by the side of a rough wickiup. The clawing red fingers of light were just streaming up from the horizon when Slick Sadman left with his men of the owlhoot trail. It seemed that this camp was not far from the upland meadow.

In the silence that fell, she tried to get rid of her bonds, but they were tight. Even as she struggled, she wondered just how far she would get from the two guards even if she did manage to free herself. In that hill country and on foot, she knew she would merely escape from one terror to another. Unless she found Dave. But her thoughts were running crazily ahead! She was not free, and Dave and the others were being attacked!

It seemed a long time that she lay there futilely trying to loosen bonds that showed not the slightest sign of slackening. But in reality it was not so long. The Mexicans busied themselves round the camp, now and then giving her a glance. They were dirty halfbreeds, and even the work they performed was done lazily.

And then came to her ears the sound of furious hoof-beats. The half-Mexicans stopped their chores and waited. Two horsemen came galloping into the little rock-bound arroyo. One was Slick Sadman and the other was his hatchet-faced sidekick.

Behind him scrambled two more horses. Both riders looked pretty grim and sort of scared. They had the grimness of men who were running for their lives.

Slick jumped from his bay and came to Mabel.

'Yuh needn't look so happy, gal. Yuh smart pal won't get me. Yuh make a pretty good hostage.'

'I see yuh left some men behind,' said the girl coolly. 'Or did they go off to the saloon in Pine City?'

'Shut yuh mouth, yuh durned hell-cat! Ef yuh want to know, that smart *hombre* is comin' thisaway, but he's coming into lead poisoning.'

There was some talk among the remnants of Slick Sadman's outfit. It seemed the six remaining

147

men were not keen to meet the three determined men riding that way.

'What's it tuh us tuh kill this galoot?' one man spat at Slick Sadman. 'Yuh always said it were best tuh beat it right back if any lawmen came ridin' into these hills. Yuh always said the hills would beat the law without us riskin' our skins!'

A grumble came from another man.

'Sure is right. These *hombres* are lead crazy. They don't give a darn. An' they're smart.'

'Yuh want to ride out on me?' snarled Slick Sadman.

'We reckon yuh should get wise and beat it,' said another boldly. 'Make up yore mind, Slick. We ain't got much time. Sure are plenty o' other territories plumb ready fer pluckin' without staying right here. Let's get outa the way o' these galoots. Yuh coming?'

'No! Durned ef I run from that gunslinger!' ground out Slick Sadman. 'I hate his durned hide! I got the gal here. He gotta be careful what he does!'

'Wal, we're hittin' the trail,' said the other deliberately, looking round at his pals for support. He saw them nod imperceptibly, and he went on: 'Adios, Slick. See yuh again, maybe, or in hell!'

There was incredulity in the outlaw's harsh face. He knew he had rodded the men too far. He could not draw back now. He felt tempted to draw his gun, but he stayed his hand.

The other renegades would shoot him down if he tried to throw for the hoglegs on his thighs.

In seconds the hellions had left their leader – proving that his leadership was held only by a straw. Such was the way of those who banded for loot and profit. Their motto, after all, was every man for himself.

Slick turned to face the oncoming horsemen. He pushed his horse well out of sight behind an overhanging outcrop of rock, and then he set himself down behind a large boulder. He pulled the girl over beside him.

'Make a sound before I shoot an' I'll smash yuh face against that rock!' he threatened.

He waited the coming of Dave, Frank and Jervis. He knew he had the advantage. They would be following the trail, and it led right into the shallow canyon. They would not see him until his gun spoke. Then it would be too late for one, two – maybe three of them. If he thumbed the hammer quick enough he could get three. But he vowed he'd get Dave Markham.

His hatred was a burning thing that had no reason.

The sound of hoof-beats was stronger now. The three horsemen were coming quickly in the right direction. There was even the sound of voices. Slick Sadman grinned thinly, and savagely. They were walking into a one-man trap.

His hopes of successfully ambushing the others

rose by leaps and bounds.

He would catch up with his pardners and re-establish his leadership – and maybe deal with the recalcitrant element later in his own tricky way!

The first horseman came into view. It was Dave Markham, his gelding picking a way through the boulder-strewn canyon. Dave carried a rifle across his saddle. Slick grinned. This was just as he wanted it. The other two men were carrying rifles, too.

They would be slow in reaching for their six-guns, and a rifle could not be brought up as quickly as a six-gun.

Slick was waiting until the range was almost point-blank. The seconds ticked off as Dave's gelding brought him nearer to the hidden outlaw. Then Slick Sadman judged his time was near. The gun came over the top of the boulder, steadied for a second, and exploded.

But even as he pressed the trigger, Mabel rolled into him! She had been waiting for the chance. She had been tense until the last moment, knowing everything depended upon split-second timing.

The bump completely spoilt the outlaw's aim. He literally cried in rage, and almost turned the gun on the girl. But at the last second he desisted.

But even as his bullet whanged wide, he had flopped back behind the boulder. He was completely sheltered – for the time being! But he knew as well as anyone that three men could easily circle one.

Dave and the others flung themselves from their horses and scrambled for shelter. They got behind rocks similar to the one that sheltered Slick Sadman.

'Stick yuh hands up and come out!' shouted Dave. 'We know yuh're on your own. We saw yore men ridin' hell for leather over yonder ridge. Reckoned yuh were with 'em.'

'I got yore gal, Markham,' snarled the outlaw. 'Right here beside me. Make a move tuh circle me an' I shoot her to rags!'

'Yuh can't stay behind that rock all day,' stated Dave. 'Come out with yore hands up. Yuh'll get a fair trial down in Pine City. If yuh got friends, yuh can get them tuh help yuh down in the city. That's a fair offer.'

'Blast yore hide, Markham!' spat the other. 'I don't trust my friends! I'm coming out – sure – but I'm going fer my hoss.'

'We'll blast yore skin off!' shouted Frank Manley in rage.

'No yuh won't, pardner. I'm leaving the girl right there beside that rock, an' if yuh show yuhself it won't be yuh that gets the slug – it'll be the girl!'

Cautiously, Slick Sadman raised his head. He surveyed the rocks ahead and chuckled. His threat had taken effect.

If one of the other men made the slightest move Slick Sadman intended to shoot the girl. He would do it because he knew it was merely a matter of time before the others encircled him. But they would not move because they dared not risk Mabel's life.

It was a tense moment for him. Sweat ran down his sallow face. In a sense it was all a bluff, for if he killed the girl, he would sign his own death warrant. But the others intended to get him anyway.

He backed step by step, gun in hand, eyes searching the rocks ahead. One false step – if he stumbled – the others would whip out guns. But if they whipped out a gun while he had everything under control, he would shoot the girl.

As he went back step by step he knew the others dare not risk his bluff. They just dared not make a move. He had every chance of getting away as long as he could keep a line on the bound girl beside the boulder.

But he reckoned without Dave Markham's swiftness with a gun! Just as it seemed he was near to his horse and could pull the animal out of the bluff, a movement came from the rocks.

A gun whipped out and, without even steadying, roared death! Slick Sadman tried to match this incredible speed with a despairing effort, and his gun actually exploded. He had aimed at the girl. But the death-dealing slug that hit him between the eyes jolted his aim. He fell backwards like a dummy from which all life had drained suddenly and dreadfully. There was still a silly and astonished expression on his face as he slowly toppled.

His bullet had bit into the rock within inches of Mabel's face. It was an ordeal which the girl endured without a cry.

Had Dave been slower or had he fumbled the shot, Slick Sadman would have taken the girl's life. There was no doubt about that. But Dave had been playing for something that meant the world to him. As he rose from the rock and went towards the girl, the strained expression etched into his face showed that the decision to make the fast shot had been no light one.

Slick Sadman was dead. A dead *hombre* who had bucked a fightin' man!

Dave caught Mabel, took out a knife and whipped the ropes from her arms and feet.

'Yuh all right, honey?'

'It's – it's – horrible – but I'm all right! At least I think so! Oh, I don't know what to think! Thank God it's over!'

'Sure is over, Dave,' said Jervis, looking at the dead outlaw. And then Mabel said:

'It was Lash Logan who took me from the ranch-house. He brought me up to the foot-hills to meet Slick Sadman's men.'

'That double-crossin—' began Jervis.

'Don't think it's over yet,' said Dave. There was

a determined jutting of his jaw that showed he lumped Lash Logan with Slick Sadman.

'Yuh can leave him to the sheriff, Dave,' said Frank, uneasy at the look on Dave's face.

'Maybe. Let's git goin'. I've got to see someone in Pine City.' And that was all they could get out of him. Frank had the unpleasant job of taking Slick Sadman's body down to the town. They wanted the body as evidence that the outlaw was destroyed.

The trail down from the hills was one that could not be hurried, and all the way Dave Markham's thoughts were sombre. But Mabel was riding the gelding with him, and he could not be moody with her. She would not let him. With a woman's sudden adaptability, she had thrown off all worries.

'I knew you'd get that man, Dave.'

'Yeah. He was plenty bad.'

'It's you an' me now, Dave.'

He smiled. One of his rare smiles that lit up his face, making it seem suddenly tender and boyish.

'That's a certainty – pardner!'

'No more troubles!'

'Maybe – some troubles!' he laughed. 'Everybody has troubles.'

She looked at him piquantly.

'Sometimes I think yuh thrive on trouble.'

'Honey, I'm a fightin' man. Yuh might as well know it. Maybe they'll make me sheriff. That'll take the fightin' outa me – maybe.'

They rode into the Double J spread first later in

the day. Mabel, despite her protests, was left there. It seemed she would be safe now.

Frank and Jervis insisted upon going with Dave to Pine City. They knew what was upon his mind. A cowboy had reported that Lash Logan was in town. He had been drinking all the other night.

They rode into Pine City as the great red sun was filling the sky with its red evening light.

The town was plenty full, but as the three horsemen came in with the dead Slick Sadman across Dave's saddle, a hush fell over the street. There was a deadly purpose about Dave's manner.

He merely dropped the body outside Sheriff Parsons' office, and then rode on.

Only a block away was the Last Chance Saloon. Even as Dave and the other two men approached, a man came out and stood on the boardwalk. It was Lash Logan. He was not drunk. He was steady as a rock. He stood staring at the three horsemen.

'Yuh two halt right here,' said Dave to Frank and Jervis. There was something in his tone that made them comply. They were grim. They knew what was in Dave's mind.

Dave dismounted and walked slowly along the street. The other man stood silent and motionless for a moment, and then, as if seeking all his courage, he moved forward a step. He came down off the boardwalk and continued along the dusty main street.

They were walking towards each other – two

grim, vengeful men. It was a custom of the West. One of them had to die, or never show his face in the town again. Dave had flung down the challenge.

As to Lash Logan, he was no coward. He had been in gun fights before, and boasted a few notches on his gun. He was a two-gun man, which is more than many a cowboy could boast.

They were still walking, and there was a stillness over the town. People were at windows, and at doors, but all out of the way of stray bullets!

The tenseness came to an end when the men were about ten yards from each other.

There was fury and hatred working in Lash Logan's face. He did not underestimate the challenge. But he was sweating. His eyes were grim slits in a brown mask.

Dave was grave and tense. He was always the same before a fight.

All at once two guns whipped from holster leather and barked a flaming challenge!

One gun was a second ahead of the other – but both men had the same chance. They had watched like hawks. They knew it was up to the other to kill.

Flame spat in the red twilight. Two explosions echoed at once – but one man dropped to his knees as if in supplication.

The man on his knees was Lash Logan!

A bullet had whipped into his eyes, taking life from him in a second.

He fell over into the dusty street and was still.

Dave looked sombrely at the body and licked dry lips. He felt suddenly that he wished he was on the clean prairie, where maybe a wind might blow and cleanse him.

But the man had deserved killing. He had accepted the challenge – unlike Slick Sadman, who had evaded the challenge with trickery.

Lash Logan was dead!

Dave walked on, seeing nothing. Then he turned, wiped his forehead, and went slowly back to his horse.

'That sure is that,' said Jervis.

It was hard, but with the death of Lash Logan, a great weight had lifted from his mind. No more blackmail. Now was the chance to live cleanly again. The past was forgotten!

And he owed his release from worries to Dave Markham. Dave was going to marry Mabel – well, good luck to him.

Jervis patted his friend on the back.

'That was a fair fight accordin' to our traditions!'

Dave did not speak. Then:

'I'm going over to see Mabel. Got to tell her we're ready tuh get married!'

'Dave, may I wish yuh the best of happiness with Mabel?'

Dave looked at the other and grinned.

'Sure. Yuh would want to any time.'